TEN-BOY SUMMER

"How are you doing on your list of dates?" Toni asked.

"I've given that up," I said evenly. "It was pretty childish anyway."

"Couldn't make it, eh? Well, for your information, I'm already up to number seven. I'm glad I'm going to win without any competition. You always were a chicken, I guess."

I know there was no way I could talk sense to her, but at that moment I also missed her more than ever. I decided that for the sake of our friendship, I would just have to get back into the contest. But what about Craig? If he found out I was going out with other guys, I'd lose him for sure. . . .

Bantam Sweet Dreams Romances
Ask your bookseller for the books you have missed

P.S. I LOVE YOU by Barbara Conklin
LITTLE SISTER by Yvonne Greene
LAURIE'S SONG by Suzanne Rand
PRINCESS AMY by Melinda Pollowitz
CALIFORNIA GIRL by Janet Quin-Harkin
THE POPULARITY PLAN by Rosemary Vernon
GREEN EYES by Suzanne Rand
THE THOROUGHBRED by Joanna Campbell
COVER GIRL by Yvonne Greene
LOVE MATCH by Janet Quin-Harkin
THE PROBLEM WITH LOVE by Rosemary Vernon
NIGHT OF THE PROM by Debra Spector
THE SUMMER JENNY FELL IN LOVE by
    Barbara Conklin
DANCE OF LOVE by Jocelyn Saal
THINKING OF YOU by Jeanette Nobile
HOW DO YOU SAY GOODBYE by
    Margaret Burman
ASK ANNIE by Suzanne Rand
TEN-BOY SUMMER by Janet Quin-Harkin

Ten-Boy Summer

Janet Quin-Harkin

BANTAM BOOKS
TORONTO · NEW YORK · LONDON · SYDNEY

RL 6, IL age 11 and up

TEN-BOY SUMMER
A Bantam Book / July 1982

ISBN 0-553-22519-7

Published simultaneously in the United States and Canada

PRINTED IN THE UNITED STATES OF AMERICA

0 9 8 7 6 5 4 3 2 1

Ten-Boy Summer

Chapter One

It was the hour before dawn. The sky behind the mountains was changing from black to gray, blue to silver. The world below lay in total silence. Then, high on a stunted pine, one small bird began to sing. As if in answer to the song, the sun came up, the sky flamed crimson, and the world burst into full Technicolor.

At Inspiration Point a lone car was parked. Two girls stood beside it, watching the sunrise with awe. With their prom dresses and long curls streaming out in the early morning breeze, they looked like ghosts from a bygone age.

The tall chestnut-haired girl shivered slightly in the chill wind. "You know," she said,

"I can't help feeling something is missing."

"You're right," said her companion. "This is supposed to be the most romantic moment of our whole high-school careers. The traditional watching the sunrise after the prom. How come it doesn't seem that romantic?"

The girl with the chestnut curls laughed. "Maybe it would be better if the boys had stayed awake."

The other girl laughed, too, and looked back at the car, where two tuxedo-clad forms lay openmouthed, snoring very unromantically.

This is probably a good time to introduce myself. My name is Jill Gardner. I am that tall chestnut-haired girl in the romantic scene. And the person sharing it with me, as she has shared all my triumphs and defeats and misadventures since second grade, is my best friend, Toni Redmond.

Let me add before we go any further that our looks are deceiving. Because I'm tall and serious-looking, everyone expects me to be the leader. But Toni, who only stands five-foot-three in high heels and *looks* as cute and helpless as a baby, can usually talk me into anything—and lead me straight into trouble! But more about that later. First back to our romantic scene on the mountain. . . .

                    *   *   *

Toni turned back from the car, a look of disgust on her face. "Boy, what a disappointment," she said. "How did we ever get stuck with those guys?"

"Habit, I suppose," I said. I was shivering in the early morning chill, and I rubbed the goose bumps on my arms.

Toni, who didn't seem to notice the cold, wrinkled her nose. "Going steady is definitely for the birds."

I nodded in agreement.

"I don't know why we thought it was such a big deal," she said, sighing.

I thought about this as my teeth chattered. "I suppose," I said at last, "it was because everyone else was doing it. We didn't want to be left out. And besides, it wasn't all bad, you know."

"I suppose they have had their moments," Toni said. "But look at them now. Do you think I'd want to spend the rest of my life with *that*?"

I had to smile. "Oh, they're not so bad when they're awake," I said. "They're polite and good dancers and careful drivers and— and—"

"Definitely boring!" Toni finished the sentence for me.

I had to agree with her. "Definitely," I said.

3

"Toni—we've got to do something right now. I don't want to be stuck with Eric through my senior year."

"And I," she said determinedly, "have definitely had enough of Scott." She kicked a loose chunk of rock so that it bounced down a thousand feet or so and disappeared into the valley. "I think it's time for us to break up with them."

"Right now?" I asked, getting a sinking feeling in my stomach. I think I must be security conscious because I hate changes, particularly quick, dramatic ones.

"Right now," Toni said.

"You mean wake them up and say 'Guess what? We're through'?"

"Well, when then?"

"How about writing them a letter?"

"Anonymous, maybe?" Toni teased. "To whom it may concern: Your girl is going with someone else behind your back and loves you not. Signed, A Secret Friend!"

"Come on, Toni. I know I'm a coward, but I'm not as bad as that. It just doesn't seem fair to let them take us to the prom and then wake them up and tell them we never want to see them again. We have to do it gently and tactfully."

4

"Like how?" Toni asked. "You know gentleness and tact are not my strong points."

Then I had one of my rare great ideas. Usually it is Toni who comes up with the touches of genius. "Listen," I said. "I've got this great idea. We'll say we're going to be so busy working this summer that we won't have any time to see them. We'll say that because we don't have much time, we don't want to keep them tied down to us. We want them to go out and have a good time dating other girls this summer, even if we are slaving away. . . ."

"I think I'm about to burst into tears!"

"Well, you think of a better way then!"

"No, Jill, I think it's great. Honestly I do. That way they'll probably be relieved they don't have to hang around waiting for us all summer. But will we really be working? At real jobs, I mean?"

"Well, I don't know about you, but I really need the money. I don't have to remind you, do I, that college is just one year away? My parents have made it perfectly clear that they will pay for the studying part but that any spending money has to come from me. I'd kind of like a car of my own and some new clothes."

"Me, too," Toni said. "So we had better get

good jobs. But what can we do? What are we qualified to do?"

"We'll think of something," I said.

"I'm glad you have the brains." Toni smiled sweetly. "I'll let you do the thinking."

"Hey, wait a minute. I may have the brains, but you have the imagination, and we're going to need a lot of that if we don't want to end up in McDonald's all summer."

Suddenly Toni gave one of her excited clutches at my arm, almost sending us both over Inspiration Point to the rocks below.

"Hey, you know what?" she yelled. "This summer is going to be fun. Getting out into the real world, dating really sophisticated men instead of shrimpy high-shool boys. And no more going steady!"

"Right!" I agreed. "I think I'll set myself a target for the summer."

"What do you mean, a target?"

"A number of different boys to date. Let's see, how about five different boys before September."

"Five? Why not ten?"

"Ten boys? That's impossible."

"Well, with your sort of personality, it might be impossible," Toni teased. "But with my magnetism and charm, I'm sure I'll have no problem. Let's make a bet on it."

"What do you mean?"

"I mean if one of us dates ten boys during the summer, then the other has to buy her anything she wants."

"Within reason," I said. I had a sudden vision of Toni in a Trans Am sports car wearing a mink coat and flashing the world's largest diamond.

"OK. Within reason."

"But what if we both date ten boys?"

"Then we both have a fantastic summer!" she yelled. She looked around. "Hey, look at that," she said. "I think the sleeping beauties are waking up."

The sun was now shining through the windshield of the car, and the two sleepers were stirring uneasily as the first sunbeams shone in their faces.

"What's happening?" Scott asked drowsily.

"Nothing much," Toni said. "Dawn just broke, and you missed it."

Chapter Two

"Well, that's that," Toni said as she swept past me into my house and helped herself to a Coke from the refrigerator.

"What's what?" I asked blankly. "And pour one for me while you're at it, will you?"

"I've done it—I'm free! I've broken up with Scott!" she said as she splashed Coke into a couple of glasses.

"Toni! You haven't!"

"I most certainly have."

"When? Where? How? Tell me all."

Toni sat down at the kitchen table and looked smug. In fact, she looked just like our cat Miranda did the one time in her life she caught a mouse.

"It was easy," Toni said. "I just went up to

him and said, 'Scott, we both know it's over, so let's not pretend anymore. We've changed. We've both matured, and now we're two different people. So let's say goodbye like two mature adults.' But he clung to me and sobbed, 'Oh, Toni, don't leave me. Life wouldn't be worth living without you. . . .' "

I looked at Toni's face. For the first two sentences I had almost believed her.

"OK, wise guy," I said dryly. "Now tell me what really happened. Did you really break up with him?"

"Of course," Toni said. "I said to him, 'Scott, I don't think I want to go steady anymore.' Then he said 'OK,' and then we went out for ice cream, and then we went home. But that doesn't sound nearly as good."

"You mean it was as easy as that? He just said OK?"

"That's right!" Toni looked smug again. "And now I'm free for the whole summer."

She took a couple of gulps of Coke, then a thoughtful look crossed her face. "But in a way it would have been kind of satisfying if he had broken down and sobbed."

That was Toni for you. She always had been the dramatic one. She told me once that she had cried so loudly when she was born that she had lost her voice on the sixth day.

Her parents had rushed her to the emergency room, thinking something terrible was wrong with her, only to find that there was nothing wrong but her bad temper.

I never quite believed this story. Toni tended to embroider the truth a little when necessary. She was also a hopeless optimist with a head full of impossible schemes. Unfortunately, it was usually up to sensible old me to try to pull her down to earth again.

More than once since I've met her, though, I've willingly taken the blame for some of her more terrible doings because they were *so* terrible that the other kids looked at me with wide-eyed respect. In fact, Toni has caused me a lot of trouble—what with her bad temper and her brilliant ideas.

I never really wanted to get involved with her in the first place. I was quite happy leading my quiet, well-behaved life. She arrived in our town for the beginning of second grade. Most of us other kids in the class had been together since kindergarten, if not nursery. When anyone new joined the class, he or she usually looked down at the ground a lot and hung around shyly in corners waiting to be asked to join the rest of us. Not so Toni. I first noticed her as I was settling into my new seat on the first morning. Our second-grade teacher, Miss Costello, was nice and let us choose seats near our friends.

"As long as there is not too much chattering when we are supposed to be working," she had said.

I had chosen a seat behind Martha and to one side of Elaine. They were both nice, well-behaved, quiet little girls like me, and we had played together since we could walk. At that time I counted them as best friends.

Suddenly a desk lid banged down on the other side of me. I looked up to see this tiny girl with green hair sitting in the seat Monica had already claimed. The green-haired kid grinned at me, revealing a mouth missing both front teeth.

"Hi," she said. "I'm Toni."

"Hi," I answered halfheartedly. "That's Monica's seat." Monica was the biggest, toughest kid in the class—the undisputed leader of second grade, and she had already chosen a seat right in the middle, where she could control everyone at once.

"The teacher said I could sit wherever I want," the new kid said. "I want to sit here. Monica can sit somewhere else."

I gazed at her in openmouthed horror— that anyone should be dumb enough not to be scared of Monica! I was scared of most things at that time, from big dogs on the way to school to big kids in the school yard— and Monica was the worst thing of all. She was huge and fat and had a face straight out of *King Kong.* She had no sense of humor, and she didn't like smart people. In fact, the smartest people stayed well out of her way! The little kid continued to sit there calmly and met my look of horror with a big, toothless grin.

Then curiosity got the better of me. "How come you have green hair?" I asked.

She laughed. "I used to swim every day in a pool. The chlorine makes my hair green. It's really blond, just like a movie star's."

At that moment Monica herself lumbered in. "That's my seat," she said, towering over Toni.

"Tough," Toni said. "I got here first."

Monica opened her mouth, but no sound came out.

Just then Miss Costello rapped on the desk for silence. "Everyone sit down," she called. "Sit down, Monica."

"I don't have a seat." Pointing at Toni, she said, "She's in my seat."

Toni looked at Miss Costello, full of wide-eyed innocence. "You said we could sit near our friends," she said, sounding as if she were about to cry. "And she's my only friend in the whole class."

And to my horror, she pointed at me.

Miss Costello smiled sweetly at her. "Well, in that case, I think Monica can find another seat," she said. "See, Monica, there is a nice desk next to Tommy in the back row."

Monica shot me a look of pure hate as she stomped to the back. I was Toni's friend whether I liked it or not.

Actually, I didn't like it one bit. I would rather have been in Monica's good books any day. Especially during recess when she called us out.

"Hey," she yelled to Toni. "If you don't give me back my seat, I'm going to beat you up."

"Try it," Toni said cheerfully. "We're not afraid to fight you."

My throat went tight as she included me. I tried to say, "I don't want to fight," but I was so terrified that no words would come out. Then I looked at Toni, frail and helpless-looking, her brave green hair coming only up to Monica's shoulder, and my deep-hidden streak of courage and loyalty was roused. Toni would not die alone!

"Yeah," I said, trying to sound brave, "we're not scared to fight you!"

Without warning, Monica gave me a hefty

13

push that sent me flying backward, showing (to my utter disgrace) my underwear with teddy bears on it.

Monica burst out laughing. "Look at her underwear!" she yelled for all the school yard to hear. "She's got teddy bears on her underwear!"

A small green-haired flying missile launched itself at Monica's middle. Punches as hard as any boy's hammered into Monica's fat stomach. Monica fell to the ground, crying, gasping, and doubled up in pain. Before we could do anything sensible, teachers and kids were all around us, and we were whisked off to the principal's office.

I was in a state of speechless terror. Going to the principal's office was something that only happened to wicked children, like going to hell. Never, in my worst nightmares, did I imagine myself being taken there. But when I glanced across at Toni, she gave me another toothless grin and looked, if anything, proud of herself. The principal looked very terrible, sitting behind his big desk.

"What was this fight about?" he asked.

"Monica was picking on that new kid," one of the witnesses said, since Monica was still sobbing and doubled up and could say nothing herself.

The principal looked at me. "Jill, I'm surprised to find you here, involved in this," he said, so severely that tears flooded to my eyes. "I always thought you were a well-behaved little girl. Were you fighting, too?"

I nodded speechlessly. The principal gave a small half-smile. "Well, I admire your bravery in sticking up for a smaller child," he said. "But please remember in the future that fighting is not a good way to settle anything."

What I actually remembered was that fighting was an excellent way to settle anything because Monica treated Toni and me with great respect after that. It didn't occur to me for a long time after, though, that Toni had let me take the blame (or the credit) for the whole fight and that she had left the principal's office with nothing said to her.

So there I was, stuck with Toni as a best friend. It wasn't so bad most of the time. She was bubbly and bouncy and had good ideas and told terrible, untrue stories and made me laugh. But every now and then, we'd both get in trouble, and I'd wonder what I had done to deserve a best friend like her when I could have had nice, quiet Martha or Elaine.

"I can't imagine how you two ever stay together," people always said about us. "You're not at all alike."

But, you know, in a funny sort of way, I think that is exactly why Toni and I have always stayed such good friends. Because we are opposites. It is as if we are both the better half of the other. Sometimes she says she wishes she were sensible and calm and a good student like me, and sometimes I wish I were reckless and imaginative and adventurous like her.

Sometimes we even envy each other's families! Toni comes from a chaotic household with a mother who is a potter and three older brothers who taught her how to punch. I, on the other hand, come from a very quiet, peaceful home. There're just two parents, both older than average, and me. My father is a lawyer, sometimes as boring as only lawyers can be, and my mother belongs to that vanishing breed of housewives who bake their own cookies and do flower arranging in their spare time.

Actually, I am not an only child. I do have a sister, Stephanie. But she is already married and lives a few blocks away. She is also already repeating the pattern of our parents with a nice suburban house, two nice children, and a life full of PTA meetings and ear infections.

Sometimes I get scared and wonder if I'll turn out just like her. Then I'm glad to escape to Toni's house and be reassured that there is a world where mothers forget to cook meals and walk around with clay in their hair and children yell at each other across the dinner table.

"So when are you going to do it?" Toni asked, bringing me back from my daydreaming.

"Do what?"

"Are you on the same planet as the rest of us?" She sighed. "What have we just been talking about? What was my major achievement?"

Light slowly dawned on me. "Oh, you want me to break up with Eric."

"Well, I certainly don't want you going steady if I'm not," she said. "We agreed, remember?"

"OK, OK," I said. "Don't get excited. I told you I didn't want to go steady anymore, and I meant it. It's just a question of choosing the right moment to tell Eric. After all, boys are very sensitive. I don't want to hurt his feelings."

"I'm sure you'll know the right thing to say," Toni said. "You always do."

She looked at her watch. "Oh, darn! Is that the time? I promised my mother I'd go to the store for her. We have nothing in the house but baked beans. If I don't buy some real food, we'll all die of starvation!"

She rushed to the front door, almost knocking over the flower arrangement in the brass pot that stood on a small, spindly-legged table in the front hall. I grabbed it and steadied it, just in time.

"Whoops!" Toni grinned.

I don't think I've mentioned yet that she is also accident-prone!

As she opened our front gate, she turned back and called to me. "You better have told Eric by the next time I see you," she warned. "Or else!"

Chapter Three

It's funny what a fine line there is between being nice and being a coward. I still couldn't decide which I was five minutes before Eric was due to arrive for The Big Showdown. All I knew was that I had a bad case of nerves.

I changed my outfit at least five times. Everything I decided to wear was wrong. The first outfit was Eric's favorite, and I didn't want to make the scene more emotional than necessary. Then I put on a pale yellow blouse that ties above the midriff. I caught a glimpse of myself in the mirror and decided that this one was *much* too sexy. Then I put on a dress my aunt had sent me once, a plain blue shirtwaist with a white belt. I knew that couldn't be too sexy because the only time I'd ever worn it my father had asked me if I was planning to become an air force nurse. But I decided it was too ugly. And I didn't want him to be *that* glad he was getting rid of me.

I was almost down to my ski clothes or my long formal. So in desperation I put on my funny T-shirt—the one that says on it, "JUNK-FOOD ADDICT: In case of collapse feed candy bar immediately."

"We'll part on a lighthearted note," I said to myself in the mirror. "Play the clown to hide my broken heart!"

"Hey, wait a minute," I interrupted myself (and you can see what a bad state I was in when I started to argue with myself!). "You're breaking up with him. You should feel elated and free."

But I couldn't help feeling sad and a little scared. After all, Eric and I had been a couple all year. People at school said Jill'n'Eric as if it were one word. We'd had some good times together, too. Granted he was a little boring when he rambled on about the wonders of the insect world, but he *was* comforting to have around. I began to panic. What if I never got another boyfriend, ever? What if I looked back on my life at eighty-one and said, "Jill, you could have been happily married with grandchildren by now. If only you hadn't thrown away your chance with Eric. You could have led a long and full life with Eric by your side for sixty-five years. . . ."

It was this last thought that brought me back to sanity again. The thought of sixty-five years of uninterrupted Eric made me decide instantly that I was doing the right thing. If he was boring at sixteen, heaven knows how he would be at eighty!

So I brushed my hair and noticed with satisfaction how it glinted in the sun. Then I put on just a touch of makeup—enough to make me feel pretty but not enough to make him feel hopeful—then I went downstairs.

The doorbell rang almost immediately. Eric was, among other things, very punctual. It went with being an eagle scout and helping old ladies across streets.

"Hi, Jill," he said.

"Hi, Eric."

"How are you?"

"Fine."

You can see the conversation was getting off to a witty start.

"Do you want to do anything special this evening?" he asked, sinking down onto the sofa and taking off his glasses to polish them—

something he does about a hundred times a day.

"No, nothing special," I said, keeping my voice calm and even. "Just talk."

He looked up from polishing his glasses and smiled. "That's good, because I really didn't want to go out," he said. "I want to watch this *National Geographic* special on spiders."

"Oh," I said. "Sounds interesting."

"Yeah," he said eagerly. "There are supposed to be some great scenes actually taken inside a wolf spider's den."

Now can you see why I was getting just a little bored with him? He'd rather look at spiders than me anytime!

Get it over with, I told myself. *Say what you have to say or you'll have to watch close-ups of a black widow eating her mate.*

I came and sat down beside him on the sofa. He had finished polishing his glasses and put them on again. As I sat down he slid an arm absentmindedly around my shoulder. I wriggled free.

"Eric."

"Mmm?"

"You and I have to talk."

"We do? Oh, well, in that case, Jill, there's

something I've been meaning to say for a while."

"There is?"

"Yeah, and I hope you won't get upset but" —big dramatic pause—"I don't feel we should go steady anymore."

"You don't?" It came out as a squeak.

He took my hands, almost as if he were proposing to me. "Now, please don't feel bad about it, Jill. It's not your fault at all. You're a wonderful girl. I've had a great time going steady with you. But I really have to start working hard now if I want that college scholarship. My parents think you're a distraction from my work, and I'm afraid they're right. I want to be fair to you, too. . . . I don't want to keep you tied down to someone who won't have enough time for you. You do understand, don't you?"

I had a stupid desire to laugh. My lips kept twitching at the corners. But with amazing control I gazed back into his eyes, just so I could tell Toni that she wasn't the only ham in the world.

"Oh, I understand, Eric," I said in a very serious tone. "Of course your studying must come first. Of course you have to get your scholarship to a good college. I understand perfectly."

He shook his head as if he couldn't believe what he was hearing. "You're a great girl, Jill," he said.

I gave him my you're-so-right smile and said nothing.

"We can still be friends, can't we?" he asked.

"Of course we'll still be friends, Eric," I assured him.

He jumped up, almost throwing me over backward on the sofa. "Great. Well, that's a relief. I was worrying about how to break it to you. I didn't want to hurt you. . . ."

He broke off as he looked at his watch. "If I hurry I can get home in time to watch my spider program there. Is that OK with you?"

I nodded. "That's fine with me, Eric."

But he was still standing there behind the sofa.

"Well, bye then, Jill," he said and leaned over to give me a quick kiss on the forehead.

I couldn't help noticing how tall he looked and how his pimples had miraculously cleared up.

"Bye, Eric," I said.

He was almost at the front door when he turned back to me. "By the way," he called, "what was it you wanted to tell me?"

"Oh, nothing," I said, giving him a forced smile. "Nothing important."

After Eric had gone, I felt unexpectedly sad. *Isn't this what you wanted?* I asked myself. *You've broken up painlessly, with no hard feelings. You're free for the summer.* But still I kept wanting to cry.

Actually I was planning a whole evening of self-pity. I had decided to go up to my room, put on some sad music, turn out the lights, and lie on my bed hugging Teddy Blue while I thought about how nobody loved me anymore. I had planned to keep that up until tears streamed down my cheeks and made the pillow all wet. I even considered writing a few poems, such as:

> What is love?
> A fragile blossom crushed
> beneath the careless foot
> of a running child.

But my plans were thwarted by the arrival of Stephanie, together with her darling children, six-year-old Andrea and three-year-old Mark.

In seconds I was trapped in family togetherness.

"And how's Grandma's little precious?" (Big kisses all over Andrea's face.)

"And how's Grandpa's big man?" (Hugs for fat little Mark.)

"You're looking well, Mom."

"Why, thanks, Stephanie, so are you."

I looked from one to the other and frowned. "You'd think you guys had been separated by a few thousand miles for the last five years," I commented, curling myself up in the big round armchair. "You only saw each other last Sunday, didn't you?"

"Why don't you go and put on some coffee for us, Jill?" my mother asked. Then she beamed at Mark and Andrea, who were busy climbing over the back of the sofa. "And if you two go with Aunty Jill into the kitchen, she'll give you some of the brownies that Grandma baked just for you!"

They stampeded at once, nearly trampling me down in the rush to get through the kitchen door first and making me swear that I would never have children. But kids are sort of like animals sometimes: as long as you keep putting food in front of them, they keep quiet. I demonstrated this scientific fact by putting the whole plate of brownies on the table in front of Mark and Andrea. They gobbled them down as if they were starving. Then I filled the coffee pot and got it started.

The kitchen door was still wide open, and I heard Stephanie say, "But, Mom, you know how I feel about junk food for the kids!"

And then I heard my mother's reply. "My brownies are not junk!"

Ah, another evening of fascinating family conversation! But tonight I was so lost in my own world that even my family couldn't get to me. Instead of the wonderful free feeling that Toni had predicted, the future seemed scarily empty when I thought about it. I couldn't help remembering how awful it had been meeting boys before Eric. I remembered being at parties and dances when I sat in a corner and hoped that somebody would notice me. Would I have to go through all that again? It was different for Toni—she could go up to anybody in the world and start speaking to him. I bet if the president of the United States was walking down the street, Toni would go right up to him and start a conversation. But not me—it took me hours to get up enough courage to say anything to anyone.

So I glared gloomily at the two monsters, who were devouring a plate of brownies with unbelievable speed, and listened to Steph talking to Mom. They were talking about me.

"What's wrong with Jill?" Steph asked.

"I didn't know anything was wrong with her. It can't be boyfriend trouble. Eric was just here this evening. He's such a nice boy— very quiet and well-mannered. A reliable sort of boy—not like that terrible Terry-something-or-other you had a crush on when you were her age. Do you remember that car he drove—?"

Steph obviously did remember because she changed the subject very quickly. "Well, what's wrong with Jill then? She's definitely moping around. Look at her face. What she needs is something to keep her occupied. If she wants a job, I've got a great idea. You remember the day camp our church is sponsoring, don't you? Well, we still need counselors for that. I think Jill would make a good counselor. She's so good with my two, and Andrea's going to be there. It might be a lot of fun for Jill—hikes and campfires and crafts. I bet she'd love it."

I winced. Had Stephanie forgotten my embarrassing stint with the girl scouts? The only person to be kicked out for flunking knot tying? The one who got a blister on the first hike and had to be carried home?

No, Stephanie, I thought. *There are many things in the world that I would rather do than spend my summer with a hundred little Marks and Andreas, teaching them how to make animal puppets out of the insides of toilet paper rolls.*

I decided to break up this dangerous conversation before they both signed me up in my absence. I poured Mark and Andrea huge glasses of milk to wash down the brownies and keep them quiet a few more minutes. Then I carried out the tray of coffee.

My mother looked up and smiled as I put down the coffee. "Thank you, dear," she said. "By the way, Steph has an idea for a summer job for you. I know you said something about wanting to find one. Why don't you tell her about it, Steph?"

So Stephanie told me while I tried to look surprised and interested and, at the same time, tried to think of an excuse to get me out of it.

"It sounds great, Steph," I said, "but actually, I already have a job sort of lined up."

"Oh—you do? Well, tell us all about it." Stephanie sat forward on the edge of her chair.

"Well, I'm not sure of the details yet," I said hastily while the wheels spun in my brain. "But I'm seeing Toni tomorrow, and she's getting them. I'll tell you all about it when I've seen her." I smiled sweetly and poured her some coffee. "But thanks for your offer," I said as I handed it to her. "I'll keep it in mind."

Now all I have to do is find a job in a hurry, I thought. *Toni had better come up with something when I see her tomorrow!*

Chapter Four

I was determined not to be outdone by Toni. On the way to her house, I thought out what I was going to say about breaking up with Eric. I was going to tell her that Eric threatened to kill himself if I left him or that he threatened to kill me in a jealous rage.

But when it came down to it, I found that I was not like Toni. I was more like George Washington—I couldn't tell a lie.

"Actually," I said, sinking into her bean-bag chair, which was less cluttered than her bed, "I didn't break up with him at all. . . ."

"What?" Toni screeched. "But, Jill, you promised. Boy, are you a traitor."

"Hey, hold on a minute and let me finish, will you?" I said before she could throw something at me. "I was going to say that I didn't break up with him—*he* broke up with me!"

Then I told her the whole sordid story with nothing spared, even the bit about how he hurried home to watch the spiders.

"That creep!" Toni exclaimed. "After all you've done for him. After you showed him that there was a life beyond the library doors!"

She wrenched open a drawer, took out two T-shirts that were both too creased to wear, and flung them into the same corner. Then she found a third, a pretty white one with a rainbow in one corner. "Honestly, Jill," she said as she pulled off her brother's old Berkeley sweatshirt and put the rainbow shirt on instead, "we've got to be more careful in the future about the kind of boys we date."

I sighed. "That's the big question that's looming over me at the moment. Where do we find *any* new boys to date? We're not even in school right now."

"When we get our jobs, of course," Toni said brightly. "We'll meet lots of mature boys when we're out in the business world."

Then she proceeded to pull the brush savagely through her blond curls, yelling, "Ow!" loudly every time she hit a tangle.

"Toni?" I asked. "Do you have any idea

how we are going to find these fantastic jobs? After all, it's already vacation. Any job openings for high-school kids are probably filled by now. The only thing I've been offered so far is camp counselor at my nephew and niece's day camp."

"Well, you're certainly not going to meet any guys there," Toni said, laughing. "Unless, of course, you go for younger men—*much* younger men, that is."

"Well, where do we start, then? I'm ready to go and willing to try anything once."

"Elementary, my dear Watson. We study the want ads in the local paper!" Toni said. Then she flipped back the last curl and rushed out of the room.

Various odd yells and scuffling noises traced her progress through the house. Then she came bounding back up the stairs, two at a time, waving a newspaper in one hand.

She promptly tore the paper apart and found the want ads.

"Here," she said. "You take this page, and I'll take the other one." For a while there was silence while we both read our pages. I read mine, as I always did, sitting neatly in her bean-bag chair. Toni read hers, as she always read everything, stretched out on her stomach on the floor.

It was very depressing reading: experienced this . . . qualified that . . . over eighteen only . . .

"How about students and housewives wanted for telephone ad campaign?" Toni asked. "It says, 'Earn good money.' "

I shook my head. "I could never do that, Toni. Imagine getting rejected that many times in one day. I know I'd develop a telephone phobia for the rest of my life."

"Well, I could do it," Toni said. Then: "Oh, no, I couldn't. It says, 'Must be eighteen or over.' Rats!"

We read on in silence. "Hey, how about part-time child care?" Toni asked.

My eyes flew open wide with horror. "Oh, Toni, that would be worse than working at the day camp. And how could we ever meet cute boys when we were stuck with little kids all day?"

"You're right," Toni said in disgust. "There's nothing in this dumb paper at all." She crumpled it up and threw it to join the clothes in the corner.

"All right," she said, a determined look on her face. "Let's forget about dumb want ads. We should start at the top, anyway. Now, Miss Gardner, answer me this: what job would you like to do if you got your choice?"

"Any job in the world, you mean?"

"Any job that an average high-school senior could do, I mean."

"Above average, if you please."

"OK, above average. What job would you choose?"

I thought about this for a minute. "Something where I don't get dirty," I said. "I hate getting my hands dirty. And I'd like to meet lots of terrific people—"

"You mean terrific boys!"

"All right. Terrific boys. I wouldn't mind being in an office—you know, filing, answering phones, that sort of thing."

"Wait a minute," Toni said, leaping up and rummaging among the sheets of crumpled paper. "I know I saw it somewhere. . . . Ah—here it is. The very thing for you. 'Dainty Fingers Secretarial Services. Temps urgently needed. Choose your own hours. Good pay.' That sounds good, doesn't it? Why don't you go try out for it?"

I looked doubtful. "I don't know, Toni. That sounds pretty professional. I bet they wouldn't be interested in high-school kids."

"It says 'urgently needed.' Maybe they're desperate. And you'd be good at that sort of thing. I can just see you as the efficient secretary: 'Oh, yes, Mr. President—the Pentagon File? I'll get it right away, Mr. President.' "

"Shut up," I said, hitting her over the head with part of the newspaper.

"Well, you'll never know if you can get the job unless you go down there and talk to them," Toni said. "Why don't you?"

"I suppose I could go along and see them," I said slowly. "That wouldn't do any harm, would it? OK. I will. I'll see them. Maybe even today, if I can get up enough courage." Then I had a thought. "But what about you? You'd never make a secretary."

"Quite right, I wouldn't," Toni said. "If anyone said, 'Take a letter, Miss Redmond,' I'd say, 'Take it yourself!' My trouble is that I was born to go straight to the top. It would have to be chairman or president or nothing. But, actually, I really don't see myself in any office job. It's too boring. I've always thought I belonged on the stage, haven't you? I think I'll find out if there are any new shows opening in town."

"It's funny you should say that," I said, without thinking. If I had thought for a minute, I would never have told her and would have saved both of us a lot of trouble. "I saw a poster as I cycled over here. They're going to be doing *A Chorus Line* at the Lyceum

Theater. I noticed it because that is a show I've always wanted to see. Maybe you could audition for it."

Then I noticed that Toni was looking at me with that wild, excited look she gets on occasion. "I'm going to find out when the auditions are. *A Chorus Line*! How fantastic! Can't you just see me?"

"Well, I don't know, Toni," I said. I was beginning to get a sinking feeling, a feeling I had had at the beginning of a lot of her crazy ideas. "I bet they only take on professional dancers," I said. "People with experience."

"I have experience," Toni said haughtily. "I've had two years of tap, remember? And I was in *The Pajama Game* at school last year."

"Yeah, but that's hardly big-time experience."

"Your trouble is that you have no ambition. How do you think Liza Minnelli got started?"

"She had a famous mother," I said triumphantly.

"Well, other big stars, then," Toni said, never admitting defeat as usual. "They got started in crummy theaters in crummy towns like this. That's how. And that's how I'm going to get started. I'll go down there and audition."

"Well, I guess it can't hurt," I said doubtfully.

"You bet it can't," she said. "I can just see me . . . overwhelming the audience. . . ."

She leaped up and launched right into "One Singular Sensation," complete with high kicks. Her foot caught the lamp cord and pulled the lamp off her dresser. As it fell it swept the rest of the junk—makeup, ornaments, and a million other things—and brought them all crashing down to the floor.

Toni paused in mid-kick, looking at the disaster area. I started to laugh. Then her mother yelled up the stairs, "Toni? What's going on up there?" Footsteps came running up the stairs toward us. "Are you all right, Toni?" her mother called again.

Then her door was flung open.

"What on earth?" her mother asked, looking at the chaos, in the middle of which the lamp lay, on its side, flickering on and off like a neon sign.

"It's OK, Mrs. Redmond," I said, feeling weak with laughter. "Toni's just practicing to be a singular sensation."

Chapter Five

I stood outside the frosted glass door and read the words Dainty Fingers Secretarial Services, Inc. for the tenth time. In the elevator coming up, I had almost lost my nerve. Elevators with carpeting on the walls always do that to me. Now I couldn't bring my hand to turn the doorknob. In fact, I almost wished I had let Toni come with me, after all.

"You'll need me for moral support and for a character reference," she had said. But I remembered Toni's "singular sensation" performance, plus a lot of other, equally impressive accidents, and decided that I was probably a lot safer without her.

The busy sound of a typewriter clattering came from behind the glass. It sounded very fast and efficient, as if Dainty Fingers herself was at work.

"Well, go on in," I said to myself. "You can't stand here outside the door all day." But neither my hand nor my feet would move.

"How are you going to face Toni if you flunk this first interview?" I asked myself. "She'll be mad if you don't at least go inside."

So I turned the knob. As I stepped into the room, I was almost eaten alive by two enormous potted plants that stood on each side of the door. Again I wished Toni were there with me. We could have made jokes about the plants being carnivorous and being fed on the people who didn't pass the Dainty Fingers typing test.

"May I help you?" said a voice, frosty as the glass, from across the room. I looked across and saw that a person had just come out of the inner office. She was one of those middle-aged women who always look as if they have just come from the beauty parlor. Every white curl was in place. And her face was a mask of makeup that looked as if it would crack if she smiled. The makeup was quite safe with me, of course. She didn't even attempt to smile.

Instead, she looked at me as if I were a cockroach who had crawled under the bathroom door.

"And what can we do for you, young lady?" she asked again.

"Oh, I've come about a temporary office job," I said. I had practiced that line in the shower about five hundred times, so it came out pretty smoothly.

"Oh?" she said, looking as horrified as if I had said I wanted to breed pigs in her office.

"You're very young for this sort of thing, aren't you?"

The way she said "this sort of thing" made it sound as if I were signing up to be a stripper or something.

"I'm going to college soon," I lied, deciding to leave out my senior year, "and I'd like some practical experience before I start on my business major." I had practiced that line, too. It sounded so convincing that *I* was almost convinced I was going to major in business. Actually, I planned to major in anything but business—but saying it seemed to work. The woman looked slightly less horrified.

"Well," she said, "we shall see what we can do for you." She went to her desk and picked up some papers. "You've taken all the office skills courses in high school, of course?"

"Of course," I said. (If one semester of typing in junior high counts as all the office skills.)

"Good. So you probably won't have much difficulty with our little exam."

"Exam?"

"Everyone who wishes to become a Dainty Fingers Temp has to pass the exam," she said. "Fill in this form and then go to room number four. On the table you will find our general knowledge and intelligence test. You have five minutes to complete it."

Along the wall were four doors marked one, two, three, and four. I pushed open the door to room number four. I had expected to find the room empty, and I jumped when a voice whispered, "Hey, how do you spell *necessity*? I can never remember whether it's two c's or two s's."

A tall, lanky, blond boy was sitting at the table. He had the beginnings of a blond mustache, and he smiled at me hopefully.

Spelling is one of my strong points, but before I could decide whether it was fair to give him the answer, a voice came over the intercom in the room.

"Mr. Gordon?" the voice of Dainty Fingers said. "Your five minutes are up now. Please bring your paper to me. You may begin, young lady."

The tall boy left, and I attacked the test paper. Actually, it was very easy for someone in the middle of high school. I was used to taking tests, pretty well up in social studies, math, and spelling. I sailed through the capital of South Carolina, the correct way to spell *opportunity*, and twenty-four percent of eight hundred-and-fifty-six dollars.

When I brought out the completed test, the boy was nowhere to be seen. *Probably been fed to the plants*, I thought. I handed my paper to Ms. Dainty Fingers, who checked it through. When she had finished, she looked at me in surprise. "You have ninety-seven percent," she said. "That's very good. Very good, indeed."

She was looking at me very hard, as if she suspected that I had thirty-six volumes of the *World Book Encyclopedia* hidden in my purse.

"Now, if you will come with me to the office machines room, you can do our typing test. Do you know shorthand, too? Pity. Most of our Dainty Fingers temps know shorthand as well as typing. Here is the test paper. Begin when I say begin and stop when I say stop."

She stood right behind me and waved a stopwatch around. I took a look at the typewriter in front of me. It was a big electric model, and I had only used one once. For a minute I panicked as I looked for the on/off switch. I was very conscious of Ms. Dainty Fingers breathing down my neck.

"You may switch the machine on," she said. "And you may insert the paper."

I would if I could find the stupid switch, I thought. Then at last I found it, and the machine came to life with a hum.

"Here is the test passage," said Ms. D. F. "Begin to type now!"

I stared at the paper and started to type:

> Mr. J. Fotheringay Pennington III alwasy always expected his emplxoyees to maifest manifest the image of diligence and respectxability xxx instilled into the

"Stop," said Ms. Dainty Fingers. She took the paper from me. "Come back to the outer office, and we can talk," she said, stalking ahead of me. I followed her. She sat down and used a blue pencil all over my typing paper.

"Your speed was nineteen words per minute, and you made seven errors," she said. "I'm afraid that is not up to the standard of Dainty Fingers."

"But I did well on the other test," I pleaded. "Aren't there jobs that don't require typing?"

She smiled, very faintly, so that the mask did not crack. "I'm afraid we don't get too many calls for people with an IQ at genius level and a typing speed of nineteen. I suggest you try some other form of employment until you improve your business skills."

I walked away with the full weight of failure hanging over me. I caught my hip on the corner of a desk. I was nearly eaten alive by the plants again. Just as I was deciding that, all in all, it had not been a very good day, I heard a voice behind me.

"I can see by your face that you didn't make it either," the voice said, and there was the same boy with the blond mustache, lounging in a chair, his lanky limbs sprawled across the hall.

"Didn't you get a job either?" I asked him.

"No, and I'm trying to come to terms with my failure," he said. "A Dainty Fingers reject! That's pretty hard to take. It makes me wonder what I *am* good for in life."

"I feel the same."

"What's your major at school?" he asked.

"Oh, I'm still in high school," I said, blushing.

"You look mature for a high-school kid," he said. That perked my ego up a bit.

"Are you in college?" I asked.

He nodded. "I'm a premed student right

now, and I sure hope I make it through med school, because I don't think I'm going to find any other job I can do. I've already been turned down this summer as a salesman in a shoe store and as a lifeguard. There's not much left, is there?"

"I guess it's McDonald's for both of us," I said, smiling.

"Hey, that's not a bad idea," he said. "Would you care to join me for a hamburger?"

"Sure," I said, suddenly realizing that this counted as my first date of the summer!

I was actually getting my wish fulfilled—I was going on a date with a college man. Not only a college man but a premed student, and not only a premed student but one with a cute blond mustache! "Eat your heart out, Eric Vanden Berg," I muttered. "Have a good evening with your spiders."

I felt very mature, worldly, and sophisticated. I was also glad that I had decided to dress up to impress Ms. Dainty Fingers. I glanced at myself in a store window as we passed by. The checked skirt, light blue blouse, and dark blue vest looked just right. Just the sort of thing a college man's date should be wearing!

He obviously thought I looked all right, too. He grinned at me as we walked down the block. "By the way, my name's Russ, what's yours?" he asked.

I told him. *Russ*, I thought. *A mature, college type of name. Much better than Eric.*

Russ came to a halt and looked around. "Now where did I park?" he asked. "Ah, yes, there we are."

I had assumed that he would have a car parked nearby. But instead, to my utter horror, he walked across to a motorbike.

"Here we are," he said happily. "Ever ridden one of these things?"

I couldn't tell him, "No, and I don't ever want to. . . ."

But at that moment I realized that a skirt was the very worst thing to be wearing. You cannot, under any circumstances, sit gracefully on a motorbike in a skirt.

Russ helped me climb on, which also was not easy in a skirt, and I rapidly tucked my skirt around my legs as tightly as I could. Then he climbed on in front of me. "Hang on tight," he called and started the motor.

"Shouldn't we be wearing helmets or something?" I yelled into his ear.

He turned around and grinned at me. "Don't worry about little things like that. I'm a careful driver." Then he screeched away so powerfully that I would have fallen off backward if I hadn't been clinging to his waist.

I never want to ride on a motorbike again as long as I live. How can they lean over like that without crashing? Even when we were going straight, it was terrible. I hated watching the houses and trees flashing past us in a blur and feeling as if I were about to fall off any second.

McDonald's seemed to have moved to another state. I could have sworn it was only a couple of blocks away, but the trip seemed to take forever, even at the speed we were going. When we finally saw that magnificent golden arch, I almost cheered. But I was so shaken up by the ride that Russ had to pry my hands loose from his waist. And my legs were pretty wobbly as we walked up to the counter.

My spirits did revive a bit after a few bites of french fries and a sip of chocolate shake. I smiled across at Russ and waited for the witty conversation one expects from a college man.

"So," he said, putting down his shake and looking at me intently, "what did you think of Saturday's game?"

"What game?" I asked innocently.

He looked at me as if I had a few screws loose.

"The ball game!" he said, horror in his voice.

"Oh, I don't know very much about baseball," I said.

"You mean you've never watched the Mariners play?" he asked.

"Never."

"But that's terrible. Do you know what you've been missing all your life?" Then he gave me a lecture on the history of baseball—every batting average, every stolen base, every home run, every no-hitter ever pitched by the Mariners. When he had fully documented the rise of the professional team, he went on to college baseball, then to the high-school team he had played on, then the Little League before that. If his nursery school had had a team, I'm sure he would have told me which kid had crawled fastest.

Somehow my food had lost its flavor. I chewed mechanically, nodding like one of those toy dogs you see in the backs of cars. Every now and then I said something intelligent like, "Yes? How interesting. Is that a fact? Amazing."

Suddenly I realized I had learned a profound lesson about life. He was just as boring as Eric because he only talked about himself and what he liked. Eric had been the same way. Surely, somewhere in the world, there must be a boy who was interesting as well as cute, I thought. But at that point I didn't have much hope.

I didn't realize for a moment that he had changed the subject and was asking me a question.

"Pardon me?" I said, shaking the glazed look from my eyes.

"Are you ready to go?" he asked, standing up. "I'd better get on home. Another big job-hunting day tomorrow."

"Oh? What job are you going after tomorrow?"

"I have no idea. But there must be something in the world I can do. I'm not an utter idiot."

He looked so depressed that suddenly I tried to cheer him up. "Why don't you go down to the ball park and see if you can sell hot dogs there? That way you'd see all the baseball games for nothing."

I hadn't meant the suggestion seriously, but I could tell from the way his face lit up that he had taken it seriously.

"Hey, that's a great idea," he said. "That's exactly what I'll do. Boy, you're a smart person. Why didn't I think of that? You want a ride home?"

I smiled my most gracious smile. "No thanks, Russ. I really live very close. The walk will do me good. Besides, if you hurry, you might make the ball park today."

"You're right," he said. "I'm glad I met you, Jill. That would be fantastic if I could work at the ball park. Fantastic!" He wandered out to his bike like a man in a trance. Then he waved cheerfully and disappeared from my life.

I gave a silent prayer of thanks as the roar of the motorbike faded into the distance. Then I walked to the nearest bus stop.

Chapter Six

"I learned a valuable lesson yesterday," I said to Toni.

"You learned to cope with failure and rejection like a mature adult?" she asked.

"No, that college men are just like high-school boys, only bigger. There's no difference really. I thought college boys would be sophisticated and mature, but this guy was just as boring as Eric. Only it wasn't spiders, it was baseball. We were talking about baseball, and he started to tell me all about batting averages and slow pitches until I nearly fell asleep. Boy, was I glad that I didn't have to date him all summer."

"What about the kissing side of it? What was that like?"

"We didn't actually get around to kissing."

"Then you can't use it as one of your dates."

"We didn't say there had to be any kissing for it to qualify as a date," I said.

"Well, there has to be some," Toni said, "or else I could walk through a restaurant saying, 'Hi, my name is Toni Redmond, do you mind if I sit next to you for five minutes?' I'd get through all ten boys in one night."

"You could just as well say, 'Hi, my name is Toni Redmond, do you mind if I kiss you?' and also get through ten boys in one night," I said.

She laughed. "Right. So we have to have some rules. From now on it has to be the whole evening on a date, and it has to include at least one kiss."

"How about if he works nights and we meet in the afternoon?"

"All right, it has to be at least two hours and include one kiss. Does that sound fair?"

"Perfectly. But I still get to count yesterday because we hadn't made the rule then."

"That's OK. I'll let you count it because I'm going to win anyway. Pass me my red blouse."

We were dressing Toni for the big audition. The red blouse had been chosen after hours of going through all of Toni's wardrobe, trying the red with blue jeans, the purple with white jeans, and every other combination.

I tried to make her be sensible. I told her that all she needed for an audition was a plain leotard. But Toni is not the sort of person you can talk sense to when she gets an idea into her head.

"I'll wear my leotard underneath, but I want to make an instant impression," she said, her eyes glowing with that dangerous, enthusiastic look. "I want everyone in the theater to turn around, and then the producer will say, '*That* is the girl I want for my show!' "

"You've been watching too many old movies on TV. Things just don't happen like that."

"You're just jealous because you don't have my dancing talent!"

With Toni in her nothing-can-stop-me-now mood, I knew it was wiser to leave her alone. Nothing would get through to her now.

Finally, we were on our way to the theater. Toni was wearing her red blouse and white jeans, with red ribbons streaming from her hair. I had to admit she looked very cute. Anybody would have to admit that she looked cute. So why did I have this horrible sinking feeling as we walked down the grimy alley and into the dirty entrance marked Stage Door?

"This is it—show biz!" Tony shouted—and nearly ran into an older man standing just inside the door.

"Can I help you?" he asked.

"I'm here to audition for *A Chorus Line*," Toni said.

"Sign up," he said, handing her a clipboard. As she returned it, he gave her a piece of paper and said, "You're number thirty-four."

He pointed us in the right direction, and we made our way, like explorers in some dense jungle, past pieces of scenery, stepping over cables. In the wings were about two dozen leotard-clad figures, all of whom looked older than Toni. They were warming up, sliding gracefully into splits and doing a lot of other things the human body was never meant to do. They all looked very professional.

Even Toni was momentarily halted in her relentless march to stardom.

"Geez!" she whispered, clutching my arm. "They all look *good*, don't they?"

I couldn't help hoping that she would lose her nerve and that we could both slink out again before anyone noticed us. But that hope was dashed as a deep voice yelled at us, "Hey, you two kids, get out of the way!"

We jumped as a young man pushed a painted archway past us and out onto the stage.

"You want it here, Bill?" he called to someone out front. Then he turned back to us. "If you want a tip from me, you better get out of here quick. Mr. Solomon doesn't like kids hanging around when he is casting. He's got a terrible temper when he gets mad." He didn't say it unkindly, and he actually grinned at Toni.

Toni drew herself up to her full height— all five-foot-one of it—and said in her Queen Elizabeth of England voice, "I am a dancer, and I've come to audition for the show. Will you tell me where I can change?"

The boy only laughed. "You don't look like you're long out of nursery school. Where have you danced before?"

"I was in *The Pajama Game* last year," Toni said, "and several shows before that. I was lead dancer in some of them."

The last time Toni had been a lead dancer was in Miss Marvel's School of Dance spring recital in the third grade. But the boy didn't know that. He looked quite impressed. "Oh—

OK. Take off your street clothes and get warmed up with the others. Are you going to be auditioning, too?" he asked me.

"Me? Oh, no!" I said, horrified at the thought. "I'm just here to give her moral support."

"Well, you can stand offstage and watch," he said, then hurried off.

"He was cute," Toni said, following him with her eyes. "Did you notice those freckles and those big brown eyes?"

I looked around uneasily. Most of the girls had finished warming up and were now talking in twos and threes, standing together, relaxed and confident. I noticed that two more girls carrying dance bags had arrived and were quickly taking off their jeans. "Toni," I begged, "why don't we forget about this? Take a look at those girls. They all know what they're doing. You don't belong here."

"Who says I don't?" Toni snapped, starting to peel off her white jeans. "With the right director, I could be just as good as any of them. I know I could. I'll show them I've got talent."

As she was talking, she got one foot caught in her pant leg and started to lose her balance. She hopped a couple of times, then put

57

out a hand to steady herself, grabbing a solid-looking window frame. The window frame turned out to be another scenery flat and was not at all solid. It teetered back and forth, then toppled over with a very loud, resounding crash. Toni and I looked at each other in alarm.

"What's going on back there?" a man's voice called from the auditorium. "Bill, are you having prop troubles?"

"I'll go see, Mr. Solomon," another voice answered.

Toni tried desperately to free her foot from her pant leg, but she had tried to take it off over her shoes, and the heel was firmly caught. I squatted down beside her to help her. But before we could do anything sensible about escaping from the scene of the crime or standing up the piece of scenery again, Bill appeared in person—a small, shriveled old man with a mass of white hair and heavy frown lines.

"All right. What happened?"

"It was only an accident," Toni said, in her most helpless, innocent voice. "I lost my balance, and it fell. I'm very sorry."

"If you don't know how to treat stage props, you don't belong in the theater," Bill growled. "Luckily for you, there's no harm done to this one, but Mr. Solomon would eat anyone for breakfast who damaged his props."

"Oh, come on, Toni, let's go home," I whispered. "You wouldn't like to work for Mr. Solomon anyway. He sounds like the male version of the Wicked Witch of the West."

"Onstage, numbers one through twelve," someone called. The girls with those numbers hurried onto the stage. Some of the other girls started doing warm-up exercises again, but Toni just stood and watched.

"All right, ladies," said another voice, and a young man strolled onto the stage. He was tall and incredibly thin, with the hollow-cheeked look of a male ballet dancer. He moved across the stage with the grace of a cat. "Now, then," he said, "this is what I want. Nice, straight line, girls. Link arms. Music, Jerome, please. And I want: jump, kick, jump, kick, pas de bourrée, kick, lunge, reach, pivot. Repeat. Got that, girls?"

He demonstrated the steps. They came out as one graceful, flowing movement. "Now, ready, everyone?" he cooed.

The girls linked arms, and at the count of "five-six-seven-eight," they began. They all looked terrific to me.

Then this deep, booming voice came from

the auditorium. "Linda and Suzanne, stay. The rest of you—thank you very much."

The rejects walked past us. They all looked upset.

Another group went onstage, and two more girls were asked to stay. Then it was Toni's turn.

"Don't go, Toni," I pleaded. "You haven't even warmed up. . . ." But she went to join the others. She stood at the end of the line. All the other girls looked the same—tall, leggy, hair tied back in neat buns. Not like Toni, who was half a head shorter and whose red ribbons still fell to her shoulders.

The man demonstrated the steps again. As the girl next to Toni linked arms with her, Toni shot me a despairing look. The pianist began to play.

"Five-six-seven-eight," the young man called, and the dancers all went into action. Eleven bodies moved with ease, in perfect rhythm with the music. One body did not. One body was half a beat behind on the first kick, a whole beat behind on the second, got her feet muddled in the pas de bourrée, did not remember to let go of her partner at the right moment, and consequently pulled them both awkwardly forward.

"Let go, you idiot," the other girl hissed as she was very nearly pushed down into the orchestra pit. By the time Toni let go, the rest of the line was already moving in the other direction across the stage, and she had to run to catch up.

"Stop, girls, stop," the young man called as he clapped his hands again.

I heard Mr. Solomon's deep, booming voice again. It was even louder than before. "I want you girls to run through that routine again. But first—you, little girl, on the end of the row."

"Who, me?" Toni asked innocently.

"Yeah, come over here."

Toni stepped forward.

"Who sent you to this audition, kid?" he asked.

"Nobody. I came by myself."

"Well, who's your dance teacher?"

"I don't exactly have one right now, but I used to take tap from Miss Marvel."

The other girls giggled.

"Young lady," Mr. Solomon boomed. "This is not Amateur Talent Night. Get out of here. Go back to your high-school plays or whatever and let us get on with our work."

For once in her life, Toni was speechless.

"Oh," she said. She threw up her head proudly and stalked off the stage. When she got back to where I was standing, she scooped up her clothes and shoes and headed for the exit. She didn't seem to notice I was alive anymore.

As she rushed blindly out of the theater, she pushed a curtain aside and bumped into the young stagehand again. Literally bumped him, I mean. He staggered backward and nearly dropped the pile of boxes he was carrying.

"Gee," he said, putting them down carefully on the tabletop and wiping his forehead, "I thought I was going to drop every single one. These are the replacement bulbs for the spotlights. I'd be done for if I broke them." He turned and looked, half amused and half annoyed, at Toni. "Do you know that you're dangerous to have around? And where were you rushing off to this time?"

"I was just leaving," Toni said, trying to sound very cool and calm. But she could not stop a tear from rolling down her cheek. The boy's expression immediately softened.

"Hey, don't cry," he said. "Solomon didn't want you, eh? Well, that's not the worst thing in the world. In fact, consider yourself lucky. He thinks it's been a good day if he makes every girl in the chorus cry at least once. He prides himself on being mean. You wouldn't want to work for him. You're still too sensitive, aren't you?"

Toni nodded. He smiled at her. "I'll tell you something," he said. "If you really want to get into the theater, go and get yourself toughened up a bit first."

"OK," Toni said and managed the ghost of a smile. "Thanks."

"Anyway, you'd be too expensive to keep," the boy said. "The other girls would want danger money to work with you!"

"Very funny," Toni said, a little of her fire returning. She went to push past him, but he took her arm.

"Listen, I want to ask you something," he said. Then he whispered something in her ear.

She took a piece of paper and a pencil out of her canvas bag, scribbled something on the paper, then handed it to the boy. "I'll think about it," she said haughtily and walked out of the theater.

Outside, we walked down the alley together, and neither of us spoke. At last I could stand it no longer.

"Toni," I said, "that was without a doubt one of the most embarrassing experiences of my whole life. I don't ever want to go through that again, not even for my best friend. Do you understand?"

"All right, Jill," Toni said humbly. "I promise. No more theaters." Then a smile twitched at the edge of her lips. "Well, at least one good thing came out of it," she said. "That cute boy asked me for a date tonight. Now we're even!"

Chapter Seven

"Listen," I said to Toni, who was lying on a mat in her backyard, lazily rubbing suntan oil over almost every inch of her body. "June twenty-first! Two weeks of summer gone and we're getting nowhere."

Apart from our two failed attempts into the worlds of business and the theater and our two dates (the boy from the theater had not asked Toni out again), we had achieved nothing so far.

"Mmm." Toni grunted in agreement as she lay back and closed her eyes.

"So we had better do something about it, hadn't we—like go out and find a job?"

"Mmmm," said Toni.

"Are you listening to me?" I asked, prodding her body with my foot.

"Sure," she murmured. "Heard every word. Must find a job. Right after I get a little sun."

"You're hopeless," I said snappily. "Well, I am going out right now and I'm not coming back until I have a job. And I bet I'll be one up in the boyfriend race, too." Then I stalked away, got on my bike, and rode.

I had no idea where I was riding or what I was looking for. I just knew that I was determined to find a job somewhere, somehow. Then, as if fate were taking a hand, I looked up, and there was a sign in the window ahead. Temporary Help Wanted it said. I locked my bike to the nearest lamp post and rushed in without looking at the name of the place.

As soon as I opened the door, I was hit by a powerful smell—of onions and stale fries and cooking grease. Then I remembered a yucky fast food place I had eaten in once, but never again. It was called Maxi's Diner. I checked round quickly and saw the name Maxi written backward on the window. So this was the same place. But even the knowledge of how awful it was didn't make me leave. After all, I didn't have to eat here, did I? And I couldn't admit defeat.

So I walked up to the counter. A girl was standing behind it, studying her fingernails. She had a lot of fuzzy blondish hair sticking out from underneath a ridiculous little pink cap and she wore a lot of makeup. In fact, she looked like something right out of "Alice," and I almost expected her to say, "Kiss my grits."

Instead, she looked up and asked, "What'll it be, honey?"

When I told her I had come about the job, she went to find Maxi. I think she smiled as she walked away.

Then Maxi himself came out of the back room. He was a huge man, who looked as if he hadn't shaved for a couple of days. He wore a dirty apron, which might once have been white, over his barrel of a stomach. He was scratching his stomach as he walked forward, looking at me. He didn't like what he saw.

"You had any experience, kid?" he growled. He sounded and looked even worse than Toni's Mr. Solomon, and again I was tempted to flee. But I remembered my vow and stayed.

"I've done some volunteer work," I said. "I've helped in the kitchen at the old people's home. I cooked at girl scout camp once. I'm strong and hard-working."

"Yeah, that's what they all say to start with," he said. "Most of them don't know what hard work is! But I'm desperate. My cook's gone to see her sick mother, and my other waitress is down with the flu. So I guess you'll have to do. You can start right away. Go and tell Patty to find you an apron and show you how to make hamburgers. I've been standing at that griddle till I'm about to melt."

Taking with me the revolting vision of Maxi melting all over the vinyl floor, I went to find Patty. She found me an apron and took me to the kitchen.

"It's easy," Patty said. "You just take it out of the box and put it down on the griddle like this. Then when one side is done, take your spatula and flip it over like this. Now you try."

Putting it on was easy, although the ice-cold hamburger spat at me when it met the hot fat of the griddle.

"Now flip it," Patty said.

I flipped. The hamburger slid along the griddle and landed gracefully on the floor.

"I'm sorry," I said, blushing.

Patty shrugged her shoulders. "Don't worry about it, honey. That one will have a better flavor than the usual hamburger Maxi serves."

Then she left me. I couldn't help feeling that I was trapped in some sort of nightmare.

I tried to comfort myself. "But at least business is slow. I'll be able to learn as I go along."

For a while I did pretty well. I made a baby burger and a grandpa burger deluxe and two hot dogs. Apart from the buns ending up a little dark where I overtoasted them, they turned out pretty much like hamburgers should, and nobody complained.

Then, all of a sudden, the orders started pouring in: two papa burgers, one medium and one rare with everything except onions, a teenburger with cheese, and two BLTs, no mayonnaise on one.

Patty poked her head through to the kitchen and yelled this at me. By the time I had found the pencil to write it down, I had forgotten half of it. Was it two papas without mayonnaise—something without onions?

"Patty?" I called hopefully. She didn't hear me until I yelled, and when I yelled, a roomful of startled faces looked up at me.

"What is it, doll?" Patty called across the room.

I made frantic signs that she should come across to me. After all, the customers might lose faith in a cook who didn't know what a BLT was. Patty shrugged her shoulders and came over.

"What's wrong, for Pete's sake? I have all these tables waiting for me to take their orders."

"Patty, I forgot what you said, and I don't know what a BLT is."

"Boy, does Maxi know how to pick 'em." She sighed, rolling her eyes up to heaven. "It's easy, just like I said: two papas—one medium, one rare with everything except onions, a teenburger with cheese, and two BLTs, one with no mayo. Got that now? And for your information—BLT stands for bacon, lettuce, and tomato."

I rushed back to my griddle and slapped on the patties. I found some bacon in the refrigerator. Since there was no way I would watch buns as well as all this, I decided the customers would just have to have their buns untoasted. So I put buns on a row of plates, turned the bacon, then turned the hamburgers. One of them—I think it was the teenburger—did its magic sliding-to-the-floor-trick again, but I was in too much of a rush to be fussy, so I picked it right up and rinsed it off. By which time the bacon had burned. So I put the patties, in various stages of redness, on the buns, flung on anything I could find in the way of lettuce, onions, mayonnaise, and pickles and sent them through to Patty.

Then I started with new bacon and served up the BLTs, just as the complaints started to come in.

"Miss, oh, miss," I heard. Then I heard Patty's answer, "I'm sorry, sir, but we have a brand-new cook."

I felt like walking out right then, but my pride made me keep going through the first day.

I can't quit my first job after a couple of hours, I thought, and I kept grimly throwing hamburger patties onto that hot, greasy, smelly griddle. Even the knowledge that I was getting slightly better at it and hadn't dropped one on the floor for at least a half hour did nothing to cheer me up.

"Well, Miss Gardner," I asked myself more than once, "how do you expect to meet any boys if you're chained to this furnace eight hours a day? Unless, of course, there is a cute public health inspector, who is following up a hot tip about you recycling hamburgers off the floor."

At eight o'clock Maxi chased out the last customer. I started to remove my grease-spattered apron as fast as my exhausted, burned, and blistered hands would let me. Maxi came into the kitchen.

Now's the time, I thought. *Tell him this job isn't for you and that you are quitting.*

"And why are you taking off that apron

before you've cleaned the kitchen?" Maxi demanded.

"Cleaned the kitchen?" I said in surprise.

"Of course. And I expect that griddle to shine!"

"Oh, come on, Maxi," Patty said. "That griddle has never shone once in all the years I've worked here."

"Well, maybe not shine," he admitted. "But I want it cleaned good—all the grease cleaned off and all the utensils washed and hung up in their proper places."

Then he went—before I could tell him what I thought of him and his horrible kitchen.

When I got home at ten, I could only grunt unintelligible words and crawl upstairs to bed. I was quite convinced that I would never go back there again.

Chapter Eight

The first thing I remembered when I opened my eyes and focused on the gray hills beyond my window was that I had not been paid for yesterday's slave labor. That was a good enough reason to go back again.

Maxi met me at the door. He looked as if he had shaved. I took that as a good sign.

"Hey, kid," he growled, "you did a good job on that kitchen last night. So I tell you what—today I work the kitchen, and you can help Patty out front. She's threatening to quit on me if I don't get her another waitress right away."

Working out front couldn't be so bad, I decided. Taking orders and carrying plates couldn't possibly be as bad as cooking hamburgers. And, I suddenly realized, I'd be able to meet all the cute boys who came in.

For a while it was a breeze. I even picked up about three dollars in tips. Then it was like the day before—everyone came in at once. And nobody was prepared to wait. . . .

"Miss—hey, miss—over here. We were here before them! Miss, I want a burger and a shake to take out and make it snappy. I have my car double-parked."

I rushed up and down like one of those little windup men you see on street corners. And however hard I rushed, it was never fast enough for the customers.

"Hey, miss—what's happened to that papa-burger?" "Hey, miss, I said rare, and this is well done." "Hey miss, you've given me Sprite instead of Coke." "Miss—I said *no onions!*"

By seven-thirty I was about ready to dump a hamburger over the head of the next person who complained. So when I heard, "Excuse me, but this is not my order," and someone pulled on my apron, I spun around, without waiting to see who was calling me.

I turned on the man in anger. "Look, I'm not a machine, I'm a person," I yelled. "I only have two arms, and I'm running as fast as I can. And what's more, I'm new here. So if your hamburger is not how you like it, that's just too bad!"

"Miss Gardner!" came Maxi's horrified voice right behind me. "How dare you speak to my customers like that? Get your things and go. I won't have Maxi's good name brought down like this."

"If you ask me, it couldn't be brought down much lower if it tried," I said. "And what's more, you can't fire me because I already quit."

I took off the apron, flung it down, and stomped out into the night. Once the chill evening air blew into my face, I came to my senses a little and realized what I had done. I was amazed, if not horrified, at myself. I had always thought that Toni was the only one who exploded and said terrible things. Now it seemed that I could explode like Toni, if pushed far enough. I brushed back my hair from my face and thought about what to do next. Go home, of course. There was no way I was going back in there to apologize, no way I was ever going to face Maxi again. I felt tears stinging my eyes as the anger wore off, and I found that I was shaking. . . .

When someone touched my arm, I jumped, my heart pounding wildly. "I'm sorry I startled you," said the voice, "but I had to come out and tell you that I was sorry."

For the first time I took a good look at the person I had yelled at. And I felt my knees go weak. He was, without doubt, the most gorgeous boy I had ever seen—even counting TV ads for toothpaste. He was tall and slim, with fantastic dark hair that waved just right and dark eyes fringed with terrific lashes. And, unlike any boy I knew, he was wearing a business suit with a striped tie. Yet he looked awfully young to be an executive.

Over our heads, the neon sign advertising Maxi's Burgers flashed on and off, spilling a rosy glow onto the damp sidewalk and making the fantastic boy seem even more unreal. I stared at him and wondered for a second if I was imagining him. But he spoke again.

"I could see you were upset, standing out here all alone. I felt so bad about it, about losing you your job."

"That's all right," I stammered. "It wasn't your fault at all. I guess I wasn't made to wait tables. I couldn't take the pressure. It was only my second day, you see—and I didn't know what I was doing. It all got too much for me, and you were the final straw. I'm sorry I yelled at you. You probably had a legitimate complaint."

He smiled, and the smile lit up his whole face so that the dark eyes sparkled. My knees went even weaker. "I was just so starving that I didn't think," he said. "I ordered a burger, and you brought me the hot dog for the next table. I happen to hate hot dogs. I should have noticed you were overworked."

"If you go back inside, I'm sure Maxi will cook you a fresh hamburger," I said.

But he shook his head. "No, that's all right. I don't want to patronize slave drivers. I'll just hold my hunger till I get home and see what was left from dinner there."

"At least you won't risk being poisoned," I said, smiling.

"As bad as that, was it?" he asked, his dark eyes flirting with me. "Well, you obviously saved me from a terrible fate. Can I give you a ride home?"

This will show you how dumb I am sometimes. I was just about to say, "I've got my bike here." I only just managed to bite my tongue at the last moment so that I made a weird gurgling noise. He gave me a funny look, so I went on hastily, "That's very kind of you. I'd like that."

"My car's just down the block," he said. I had visions of a white convertible, or a black

Porsche, perhaps, to go with the suit. But instead, he stopped by a very old VW bug. So old that it had a small rear window. They stopped making those before I was born.

"This is Bessie," he said. "She may not be a beauty, but she gets me to and from school reliably every day."

"Oh, you go to school?" I said, surprised. "I thought from the way you were dressed you must be in high finance or government or something."

He laughed, and his eyes crinkled so fantastically that I felt like a large puddle of Jell-O. "Not too many people I know become governor or chairman of IBM at eighteen," he said.

I blushed at my stupidity, but luckily the darkness hid my hot cheeks.

"No, actually, I'm only just out of high school," he said. "I'm going to be a freshman at State this year. And the suit is because of my vacation job. Don't laugh, OK? Everyone in my family keeps teasing me about it, but I'm working for a modeling agency. It pays very well, and it's not hard work. All I have to do is stand there and look serious and distinguished, like this." And he leaned against his car in a wonderful, elegant pose.

"Wow!" I said. "What are you modeling for—TV commercials?"

"I wish," he said. "But they don't get much of that sort of work in Seattle. That's mostly done in L.A. or New York. I've just been doing things like catalog work and today a magazine photo for a new restaurant—'The Rendezvous Room, Where the In-Crowd Dines!' That's why I'm wearing this suit."

He unlocked the door for me, and we jumped into the car. Bessie's engine started with a pleasant hum, like a fat bumblebee, and we drove off.

I sat there in a dream beside him, surrounded by a rosy glow. Every time I turned to look at him I saw those fabulous lashes, curling out of his dark silhouette. Once he caught me looking and smiled at me. As we drove he talked. He had a deep, smooth voice to match his looks. He asked me about school, told me about his own plans, about being torn between becoming an accountant like his father or going into acting, which his parents thought was too risky.

I was interested. I was even fascinated, but I could not keep my eyes open. The two days of exhaustion, plus the emotional strain of the final fight, were beginning to catch up with me. I fought against the sleep that was threatening to overpower me. . . .

"What books do you like to read?" he asked, after I told him I liked reading.

"Oh, I like Robert Heinlein," I said. "Most science fiction, but Robert Heinlein especially. He has such clever eyelashes." I had meant to say "ideas," of course, and I corrected myself immediately. I explained about being so tired that I couldn't think straight. I think I saw him smile. But I don't know for sure. He might have thought I was a complete idiot.

After that I didn't trust myself to say too much more. I stared hard at the road ahead and answered his questions with one-word answers. He must have thought I found him boring or that *I* was terribly boring, or just plain dumb.

"Which is your house?" he asked.

I came back from far away to find that I had fallen asleep after all and my head had slipped onto his shoulder. I sat up hastily, feeling embarrassed and stupid. I murmured thanks and got out.

It was only as Bessie rumbled off into the darkness that I remembered two important things: one, and most important, I didn't even know his name. And two, under the rules of my contest with Toni, I couldn't even count this as a date!

"Jill Gardner, world's biggest dummy!" I reproached myself. "You meet the most gorgeous boy in the world, you say weird things about eyelashes to him, you fall asleep in mid-conversation, and you don't even find out his name—or tell him yours."

I opened our front gate. Friendly light streamed out through the glass window on the front door. I tried to console myself with the fact that at least he knew where I lived. If he wanted to see me again, he'd be able to.

The drone of the TV set came from the living room. It sounded more like the public channel type of program that my father liked than the police drama my mother always chose. I pushed open the door and saw that I was right. My father was sitting there, totally absorbed, as a man explained about inserting plastic valves in open heart surgery. My mother, not at all absorbed, heard me right away and jumped up.

"How was your day, dear?" she called, as she always did.

"I'll tell you in the morning," I said. "Right now I'm too tired to breathe, so I just wanted to let you know I'm home and I'm going to bed."

"All right, dear," my mother said. I turned and left the open heart behind me. "Oh, by the way, Jill," my mother called after me. "There was a message from Toni. She said to tell you she's become a maid."

Chapter Nine

Next morning I woke at dawn, feeling refreshed and ready to go. Above all, I couldn't wait to call Toni. I had to tell her all about my fantastic dream boy of last night (whose name I unfortunately forgot to get) and also to find out about her mysterious message. Toni couldn't have meant it for a minute. She was the last person in the world to become a maid or to do anything that involved hard work. It must be just a joke.

"Hi, Mrs. Redmond," I said cheerfully, "this is Jill. Is Toni up yet, please?"

"Oh, hi, honey," came her voice—always vague-sounding until she had had several cups of coffee. "I'm afraid Toni's not here."

"Not there? But it's only seven-thirty. I've

never known her to get up this early if she didn't have to."

"Ah, but she did have to. She has to be at work by eight. She'd gone before I got up this morning."

"You mean, Toni's actually gone out and got herself a real job?"

"Yes, wonders will never cease, will they?" Mrs. Redmond laughed. "Now, if only I could persuade the boys to go out and get some useful employment, I could get back to my pots."

"Toni left me a message about becoming a maid. She didn't really mean that, did she?"

"Sounds incredible, but it's true."

"Where's she working—in a motel or something?"

Mrs. Redmond laughed again. "Nothing so humble. You know Toni and her big ideas, don't you? She went to one of these big, exclusive domestic agencies and came home with a job as a housemaid in a mansion on Hunter's Hill."

"Toni, a housemaid in a mansion? How on earth did she manage to get herself into a job like that?"

"Knowing Toni, I'd say she probably did a good acting job."

I laughed. "But why would she want it? It

sounds like hard work, and that's not the typical Toni at all."

"Search me, honey. I'm sure she has some weird motive, but you'll have to ask her yourself. She gets home around seven-thirty tonight."

I promised to cycle over around seven-thirty and was about to hang up when she asked, "By the way, how is your job going? I hear you are working in a restaurant."

"Not exactly. It was a greasy spoon hamburger joint, and I quit. He wanted me to do four people's work."

After I hung up, I remembered again that Maxi had not paid me. Would I ever have the nerve to go back there and ask for it? Pondering this matter, I walked into the kitchen to get myself a cup of coffee. My father was sitting there, still in his robe, eating a bowl of some revolting high fiber, low-everything-else cereal that tasted like sawdust but that his doctor had recommended.

"Hi, honey," he said cheerfully. "All ready for work?"

I decided to tell him the whole story. After all, he is a lawyer, and not many people can get free advice from their lawyers. He listened patiently, nodding now and then.

"So I don't know whether he'll want to pay

me anything at all, after what happened," I finished.

My father put down his spoon. "You deserve your money, Jill. You worked for two days, you should be paid for two days." He looked at his watch. "I tell you what. I have to drive in that direction this morning. You can come with me, and I'll help you collect."

"Would you, Dad? You're the most wonderful father in the world." I jumped up and flung my arms around him until I nearly choked him to death. I might have parents who are old-fashioned and boring, but at least they are there when you need them, and that's what counts!

That morning I went in ahead and faced Maxi.

"I've come to get the money you owe me," I said, sounding more brave than I felt.

"Money? What money?" he yelled. "I don't pay people who are no use to me, who insult my customers."

"But I worked for two days," I said. "You owe me two days' pay."

Just then my father came through the door, dressed in his nice gray business suit, and handed Maxi his card. As soon as Maxi saw the name of a law firm, he went to the cash register and handed over the money like a lamb. Then I collected my bike and rode home. At least I had earned forty dollars this summer.

That evening I was at Toni's house waiting for her grand entrance after a day of playing maid. When she finally arrived, she staggered in, looking as tired as I had felt the night before.

"Just point me to the nearest chair," she murmured, then sank into it. "Do you know how many miles I have walked today—up and down stairs, along corridors, in and out of kitchens? Hundreds of miles. Maybe even thousands!"

"I'm disappointed," I said. "I thought you'd be wearing a cute little black dress with a frilly apron like maids wear in the movies."

"Most amusing," she said bitterly. "If you must know, I have to wear white overalls. They're three sizes too big for me, and I look like an attendant at a mental institution."

"What I'm dying to find out is why you ever wanted a job like that! I can't imagine you being humble and lovable and saying, 'Yes, ma'am. I'll fetch it right away, ma'am.'"

"I'll tell you the whole sad story," Toni said. "I met this girl who was a maid. She was German, I think. Anyway, she was big and blond and healthy-looking, and she spoke with a funny accent. I met her at the bakery, actually. She was buying jelly doughnuts—"

"Oh, come on, Toni. Do the jelly doughnuts have any relevance to this thrilling story?"

"Wait a minute. I'm getting to it. So anyway, we started talking, and she said she was a maid. And she told me how fantastic it was and how the family was away most of the time and she could have her friends in for parties and help herself to the family's food. Well, it sounded good, and I was beginning to get interested when the clincher happened. This white Mercedes sports car drove past, and someone honked at this German girl. She waved and laughed—and then she said that it was a couple of boys from the street where she worked and what good times she had had with them. Well, that did it. I went straight down to the domestic help agency she had been to, and I signed on."

"And?"

"And I thought I had really struck it lucky because they sent me to a family with an eighteen-year-old son. I could just see myself, mingling with the jet set, but I guess it didn't turn out like that."

"He wasn't home?"

"Oh, he was home all right. But he's an obnoxious little creep with pimples, called

Cecil, if you please. And he orders me around like I was dirt. And so does his mother. They have all this money, but they are too cheap to hire enough maids. So they expect me to work in the kitchen, make the beds, sweep the floors, fetch and carry. . . . I tell you, Jill, I feel just like Cinderella. Oh, and the worst of all, there's this woman in the kitchen, straight out of 'Upstairs, Downstairs.' She orders me around, too."

"Poor Toni! It sounds terrible," I said. But I couldn't help smiling at visions of Toni being ordered around by a pimply creep, his mother, and someone who looked like Mrs. Bridges.

"You don't think it's terrible at all. You think it's funny," Toni said in a hurt voice.

"No, I don't," I said seriously. "But why don't you quit if you don't like the work?"

Toni shrugged her shoulders. "I keep hoping that Cecil the creep will bring home some exciting friends and they'll notice me scrubbing the stairs and whisk me away to a better life!"

Which reminded her that I hadn't told her my own piece of shattering news. I made it short because I could see she was tired. But when I told her that I had forgotten to get his name, she shot wide awake again and glared at me.

"Jill, how could you? When I meet a cute male, the first thing I say is, 'Hi, my name's Toni. What's yours?'"

"Well, these were not normal circumstances. For one thing, I had almost thrown a hamburger in his face, and for another, I was so tired I didn't know what I was doing."

"Well, you're one up on me anyway," Toni said. "Two boys, even if one of them was the mysterious Mr. X."

"Well," I said hesitantly, "I can't really count him as a date, under our rules, since he didn't kiss me. I fell asleep with my head on his shoulder, though."

"Jill, you're hopeless! You've got to do better than that. Just wait until my next date."

"Toni, I think we're losing our minds. Why don't we call the whole thing off?"

"Are you kidding? I've got my prize all picked out. Don't be dumb, Jill. Don't you want a little adventure in your life?"

"I guess so." I sighed. "I guess so."

Chapter Ten

One week later Toni got a date—and lost her job. She told me afterward that she had had a catastrophic day in which everything that could go wrong did go wrong. First she was told to clean the silver. She used what she thought was silver polish, only it wasn't, and it turned all the silver black. Then she had to serve at lunch, and she dropped a chicken leg, covered in rich mushroom gravy, right into Mrs. Whatsit's lap. Mrs. Whatsit was wearing pale blue silk at the time and was not amused.

So Toni was fired. The young master did not plead on her behalf. Instead, he yelled at her to iron his shirts before she went. Toni said no in a most unladylike way and made one of her dramatic exits. Then on her way out she met the gardener, who just happened to be this really cute boy who worked for his father's landscape service, and she ended up the day on a date with him. A real date, that is, so Toni told me.

So there we were. The summer was slipping away, Toni had had two dates, I had had one, and neither of us had a job. There hadn't been any phone calls from my Mr. X, either. Every day I couldn't bear to leave the house in case he called. Every time a VW drove by, I jumped a mile. But it was never him. As the days slipped away, I began to face the reality of the situation.

OK. He was a very nice boy, I told myself firmly. He was probably a boy scout, and driving me home was his good deed instead of walking an old lady across the street.

I tortured myself a little further. He probably already had a girlfriend—a well-dressed, sophisticated model with yards of blond hair and hundreds of even white teeth. And even if he didn't have a girlfriend right now, he certainly wouldn't be interested in a moron who yelled at him, then said "eyelashes" instead of "ideas," then hardly spoke to him and fell asleep while he was talking.

My depressed mood was not cheered when

Toni met a guy from our biology class in Safeway and went to the movies with him, putting her one more ahead in the date contest.

"Why are you spending your whole summer moping around the house?" my mother asked. "If you want to earn some money, the Kleins still need a babysitter for Jackie and JoJo."

I shuddered. I remembered the last—and only—time I had sat for Jackie and JoJo. Their mother's last words to me were to "give them anything they want to make them happy," and what they wanted most was to throw ice cream at each other and at me. No, sir, I would have to be a lot more desperate before I babysat for them again.

"Then why don't you go down to the pool or call a friend to play tennis?" my mother kept on. "It's not healthy to sit here staring into space all day."

"I was not staring into space. I was watching a soap opera. Did you know that Phyllis is about to divorce Marvin because Marvin's son by his first marriage has become Phyllis's stepfather by marrying her mother? Fascinating, isn't it?"

My mother sighed and walked out. She knew I was making fun of her because she is addicted to soap operas. I felt bad about it afterward. After all, I shouldn't take out my frustrations on my nearest and dearest.

Then, in a flash, the whole scene changed. Toni, of course, was responsible. She breezed in one Wednesday, looking more enthusiastic and excited and bouncy than usual. I looked up from watching a game show and eyed her with suspicion.

"Come on, get your roller skates on. We're going," she said.

"Roller skates? What are you talking about? I gave up roller skating when I was ten."

"Well, you're going to take it up again! You and I are going to skate our way to fame, fortune, and romance!"

"We're going to join the roller derby?"

"Very funny. But you'll stop laughing when you see this!" She handed me a clipping from the newspaper: WANTED FOR NEW DRIVE-IN. ROLLER-SKATING CARHOPS. RELIVE THE FIFTIES.

"Roller-skating carhops? Are you crazy?" I asked in amazement.

"Yeah, how about that? Don't you think that sounds exciting? Imagine us in those cute little outfits, skating up to all the boys. We'll get our ten dates in no time at all."

"Toni!" I said.

"Let's go down and get the job right now—"

"Toni!!" I said again.

"And all the terrific guys from all over town will come because it's new and—"

"Toni!!!" I yelled.

She stopped. "Did you say something?"

"Yes, I did. Before you go on making plans for our fantastic future, there's one thing you ought to know. I can't skate."

"You what?"

"I do not know how to roller skate."

"But everyone in the world can roller skate."

"Everyone except me."

"But I remember you had a pair of skates once."

"Correct. I still have them, somewhere in a closet. But I never learned how to skate. What happened was that I started to skate with everyone else. Then I fell over and sprained my wrist. After that, I sort of lost my nerve. So I never really learned to skate very well. Certainly not well enough to glide around with a tray full of food in one hand."

"Oh, come on, Jill. I know you can do it."

"Look, you go get the job if you want to. No one's stopping you."

"But it won't be any fun unless you're there, too. Think how great it would be, making jokes to each other as we passed with our trays. And we could double date! Oh, come on, Jill. We both need a job, and this one could be fun. It would be better than baby-sitting, wouldn't it? And better than Maxi's? I bet I could teach you to skate in a couple of hours. We even have a spare pair of skates your size at home."

"I don't know, Toni. I don't feel good about this."

"I tell you what. If I can't teach you in a couple of hours, we won't go. OK?"

"OK," I said, sighing. For a tiny person, Toni can be a very big bully.

We went to her house, and, unfortunately, she did have a pair of skates that fit me. For the next two hours, she was the enthusiastic teacher, and I was the reluctant student.

"Hold my hands," she instructed. "Left, right, left. Glide more, bend your knees. You don't have to grip my hands so tightly. You're crushing my knuckles!"

"When I am standing on little rolling wheels, I have every right to grip your hand as hard as I like."

Then she made me go alone, and I fell down.

"That didn't hurt," she said as she hauled me up like a sack of potatoes.

"It wasn't your behind!"

But it really hadn't hurt much, and as soon

as I realized I could fall without hurting myself, I began to feel much better.

So there we were at three o'clock—skates in hand, standing outside the Oasis Drive-In. It was a gaudy, round building with a lot of neon signs, all ready and waiting to flash.

"It looks like it belongs in 'Happy Days,' " Toni said, grinning.

At that moment the owner appeared and scowled at us. He looked as if he could be Maxi's brother, but that didn't stop Toni. She was as fearless as ever.

"We've come about the jobs," she said, smiling.

Maxi's brother grunted. "Ever worked in a fast food place before?"

"I have," I said, and I immediately wished I hadn't said it. What if he asked me for references or called Maxi about me?

But he only grunted again. "What about you?" he asked Toni.

"I skate very well," she said.

"Hmmph," he said, looking at both of us as if he thought we would be useless.

"Well, if you don't need us," Toni said brightly, "we have a couple of other job interviews lined up for this afternoon. Come on, Jill." She turned away dramatically. Even I, who had known her all these years, had to admit she was pretty good.

"Hey, come back here," the owner yelled. "I never said I didn't want to hire you. But I expect hard work when you're here. No flirting with boys. No fooling around. Understand?"

"Yes, sir," we both said together.

"Be here at nine o'clock tomorrow. The uniforms should have arrived by then."

"Thank you, sir," Toni said. I just smiled, and we walked away, slowly and with dignity.

The moment we turned the corner we flung our arms around each other and went wild.

"We did it, we're hired!" we yelled.

"Jill," Toni said when we had calmed down, "this is going to be the start of a beautiful summer."

Chapter Eleven

Being roller-skating carhops at the Oasis was fun, just as Toni had said it would be. It really wasn't hard work carrying trays when we could skate up and down with them, and I even got a lot better at skating. At least, I could go forward pretty well. I still had trouble with the corners, but I made sure I always took a straight line between the counter and the cars.

The Oasis received lots of good publicity because it was new and different. One night we even got our pictures in the paper—Toni with a big smile, me looking grimly serious as if I were determined not to fall over.

Then one night our wishes came true. Two really cute boys pulled in to the drive-in, started talking to Toni, who served them, and invited us both to the movies with them. Their names were Gary and Peter, and they had just graduated from high school. They seemed like a lot of fun. We went to a great scary movie about a hand that is cut off a horrible monster and keeps crawling through open windows to strangle people all by itself.

After the movie, we drove up into the hills. The boys parked on a deserted road and produced a six-pack of beer.

"What's the matter with you two?" they asked in horror when we said we didn't drink. "Are you both babies just out of Sunday school?"

But we still refused and just sat there uncomfortably while they drank.

"I think maybe you'd better drive us back while you can still see the road," Toni said.

"Oh, come on," Gary said, slipping an arm around her shoulder. "We're not going anywhere until we get to know each other better. You know what I mean?"

"No way," Toni said. "I'd rather walk back."

"Oh, come on, baby," Peter crooned, putting his arms around me like an extra-large octopus. His eyes were glassy, and his words came out all slurred, and his beer breath was only inches from my neck. It was definitely time to get back to town.

"Drive us back, please, Peter," I asked sweetly, trying to appeal to his better nature, if he had one.

"Hey, why can't you be friendly? I thought we were really getting along. Don't worry, we'll drive you home soon," he said.

"Listen—if you don't drive us home right this minute, you'll find out how unfriendly we can be," Toni said. She was at least a foot shorter than he, and he must have weighed fifty pounds more than she, but Toni could sound pretty fierce when she wanted to.

But the boys only laughed and started in with the octopus grabs again. With the sort of telepathy that comes from years of close contact, we both exchanged glances, nodded, then caught the boys off guard with quick jabs of our elbows into their ribs. Then we got out of the car and ran. It was a long way back to town, and it was one o'clock in the morning before we got home.

I was still shaking with fright. Toni was just plain mad.

"Those jerks!" she fumed. "Those utter nerds! Creeps! Worms! To think we could have been taken in by them. To think they came across like nice, ordinary boys!"

"Look, Toni, the point is we were lucky to get away from those guys. We've got to be more careful. We can't take chances with guys we don't know just for this stupid contest. In fact, I still think we should call it off. I'm starting to feel like a real nerd myself."

"Speaking of the contest," Toni said suddenly, "does tonight count as a date or not?"

"Definitely a date. Peter planted at least one slobbery kiss on my neck, and while you were wrestling with Gary, I think his lips met yours."

"Even if they hadn't, we sure deserved to chalk this one up," Toni agreed. "That makes me four and you two. I'm nearly halfway. You'd better hurry up."

"You mean you won't agree to call if off?"

"Oh, come on, Jill. For once in your life, you're doing something halfway exciting. You can't chicken out now."

She talked me into it again, of course. But after that night, I was really depressed. I hadn't had one really enjoyable date all summer. The only boy I ever wanted to see again hadn't called me. I'd waited patiently, I'd prayed and hoped, but he was gone forever. A bleak future stretched ahead of me. After that scene in the car, I was scared about dates with strange boys. Would I ever dare go on a date again with someone I didn't know?

So who was I ever going to date? I asked myself. I supposed I could always date some old school buddies, just to catch up with Toni. After all, boys I had known since kindergarten would be safe enough, I guess, but probably not any fun. Why, oh why, did I ever let Toni talk me into this?

Of course there was the question of where to meet old school buddies. Most of our waking hours were taken up with the Oasis. Then one evening fate played into my hands. Randy Johnstone drove into the Oasis in his father's pickup truck. Good old Randy Johnstone! He had really liked me in junior high. He had grinned at me in math and even eaten his lunch beside me—and that had been pretty serious to me back then. Most important of all, I knew I could trust him.

I had just picked up a large order at the counter when Randy drove in, so I put on speed to get it delivered so I could take Randy's order. Then I saw Toni's face as she noticed Randy. I also remembered that he had taken her to the freshman dance in high school!

"See who just drove in?" she called, grinning. "That's number five for my list."

"No way, José," I said. "That one's reserved

for me. He used to carry my books for a whole year of junior high."

"So what? He took me to the freshman dance."

"So? I saw him first."

"No way."

"Well, I'm going to take his order," I said, "because my car is right there and yours is way across the lot!"

"That's what you think!" Toni yelled. "I always was a better skater, remember?"

And she set off at an incredible pace with her loaded tray balanced expertly and the shakes swaying gently in the breeze. I set off, too, cutting between two cars to get to the yellow Datsun. As I said before, I still had not got the hang of corners. As Toni flashed in front of me, I meant to turn, but my legs somehow kept on going. Toni and I met in the middle of the parking lot with a resounding crash. Hamburgers rose into the air like flying saucers. Shakes oozed over cars, and everything was littered by a hail of french fries.

We staggered to our feet and looked at each other in horror.

"You look pretty cute with that strawberry shake in your hair," I said, beginning to smile.

Then we both burst out laughing and couldn't stop.

Unfortunately, Mr. Petrini didn't think it was so funny. Quite a crowd had gathered around our little disaster area, and he came out of the kitchen to see what was going on.

"What did I tell you about fooling around on the job?" he yelled at us. "Look at the mess you've made. Get out of here. You're fired. Both of you."

"But, Mr. Petrini—" Toni pleaded.

"No buts. I don't want any excuses. Just get out. And you pay to have these uniforms cleaned before you send them back, you hear? Now get." And he stomped away.

"Looks like we're out of another job." I sighed. "Now will you call off this stupid bet? It's making us act like real jerks. We never would have acted so ridiculously over a boy before—especially a boy that neither of us even really cares about! Pretty soon we'll be batting our eyelashes and pretending to be brainless just to get a date! This is getting pretty darn degrading, Toni."

"What's wrong with you? I thought you thought this was funny," Toni snapped.

"I did, but I don't now. I feel really humiliated."

"Degrading? Humiliating? Thanks a lot,

Jill. You want to know what I think? I think you're just the most hopelessly boring person I've ever met! And I'm tired of trying to give you a little personality and adventure. From now on you're on your own! But don't think I'm giving up the contest. I plan to collect those designer jeans you're going to owe me."

"But, Toni, wait! What about our friend-ship? You can't let it be destroyed by this silly contest. Wait!"

But she just walked away, and that was the last I saw of her for weeks.

Chapter Twelve

"This summer has been one uninterrupted disaster," I told my sister. I had finally decided to talk to her because she was the one person who had time to listen.

She smiled when I told her about all the disasters—the hamburger calamity, the dream boy who never found out my name, the wrestling match in the car, and the strawberry shake collision. I ended with my fight with Toni. That one was the most painful to tell.

"If I had five dollars for every time in your life you've had a fight with Toni, I'd be driving a Mercedes by now instead of a five-year-old station wagon," my sister said.

"But this time was different," I said. "We're not little kids anymore, and we both said some terrible things we shouldn't have."

"Well, I wouldn't worry about it too much," Steph said. "I bet she'll call and apologize now that she's calmed down."

I shook my head and sighed. "Even if she does, we won't get our jobs back. I can't face the summer with no best friend, no boyfriend, and no job."

Steph got up and handed me the plate of cookies. "There's always the job I offered you," she said. "We're still short of counselors at my day camp. It's not bad money, and all you have to do is keep little kids entertained. And at least you'd have your evenings free!"

"All right," I said. "I'll take it."

So there I was, a few days later, dressed in a large white T-shirt that said Camp Chickadee Counselor on it, standing in the middle of a bunch of little kids, and feeling as if I had strayed into Munchkin land.

The first day went pretty well. We made leaf prints without covering anyone in paint. We made peanut butter and jelly sandwiches for our lunch without covering anyone in peanut butter and jelly. We played hide and seek without losing anyone. Then late in the afternoon I took my group for a nature hike. By this time, the strain of having to cope with twenty six-year-olds was beginning to show. The air seemed to resound with high-pitched giggles and screeches.

So this is it, I thought, stomping along in a cloud of gloom, a whole summer of giggles and stupid questions. How should I know why owls sleep in the daytime and why cats don't get goose bumps? This is going to be the only kind of conversation I'll have all summer. And as for meeting boys. . . .

I didn't know what to do about the contest anymore. I still didn't like what it was doing to Toni and me. But I thought that maybe if I went through the motions of keeping up the competition, she would want to be friends again. I sure missed her. And I realized now that I must have really hurt her feelings by saying how degrading the contest was (even if I was right), since it had been her idea and she was enjoying it so much. How could I make her see what I meant without making her hate me? I tried calling her once, but she wouldn't come to the phone. That was just as well because I had no idea what to say to her anymore.

"Jill, hey, Jill?" Munchkin voices called to me. "Can we wade in the creek here? Our feet are hot."

I looked doubtfully at the creek for possible hazards. But it seemed safe and shallow.

"Our other counselor let us," one of the little girls said sweetly.

My own feet were hot, too. "OK," I said, "but you better put all your shoes into my backpack so we don't lose any."

Soon we were walking blissfully along the creek while the cool water splashed over our toes. We made a dam of rocks and talked about beavers and dragonflies. It was a very nice time for all of us, and everyone was sad when I looked at my watch and announced that we had to go.

"But your parents will all be waiting for you," I told them as they pleaded to stay longer. "They'll get worried if you aren't there. And besides, you want to show them your beautiful leaf prints, don't you?"

Then I led them up the hill like a flock of sheep.

When I emptied the shoes out on the picnic table, I realized that I had made a terrible mistake. I was staring at twenty pairs of identical sneakers. I picked up a pair and tried to force them onto the feet of the nearest child. The child immediately wailed, "These aren't mine," and burst into tears.

"Well, whose are these then?" I asked, holding them up.

Blank faces looked at me. I realized I had a

problem on my hands. One kid began to cry. "I want my own shoes." And another warned me, "My mommy will be mad if I come home with someone else's shoes!"

Desperately I matched up the biggest-looking pair with the biggest boy, but after that, most of the other shoes were about the same size.

"No, we can't go home without shoes," I said, trying to keep calm. "All of you sit down and put on a pair of shoes. If they're not the right ones, your mother can tell me in the morning, and we'll change them then."

"But I want my own shoes *now*!" wailed one little girl.

"Me, too!" whined her friend.

A hand tapped me on the shoulder. "Excuse me, can I pick up my sister now?" a voice asked.

"Will you please wait a minute?" I snapped. "We've got a problem here. The kids can go as soon as they've all got shoes on." Then I turned around to glare at the person.

"OK, but I can't figure out why you start yelling whenever I open my mouth," he said. It was my mystery dream boy!

I stared at him, open-mouthed. "What are *you* doing here?" I stuttered. For one wild moment I hoped he had tracked me down.

"I came to pick up my sister," he said,

pointing at the sweet little girl who had asked me why cats didn't get goose bumps. "But what are *you* doing here? Last time I saw you, you had just walked out on a promising career in the hamburger business!"

"Very funny. But I'll tell you something— children are much easier to handle than hamburgers."

"I'm surprised at that," he said, grinning. "I'd trade Cindy in for a hamburger any day!" He ruffled her hair and she glared at him.

I took a quick peek at her name tag. "Cindy Wexler." Well, at least I knew his last name now.

"So Cindy's your sister?" I asked.

"My youngest sister. I have four of them, ranging in age from six to thirteen. I'm the only boy. My name's Craig, by the way. I forgot to mention it the last time we met. In fact, I forgot to find out your name, too. Very dumb of me, but I guess we were both tired that night."

"I'm Jill Gardner," I said. We smiled at each other as if the twenty Munchkins had vanished.

But they soon made us aware of their existence again. "Jill, I want my shoes!" "That's my mommy over there." "I want to go home now." I came back to reality with a bump. "Oh, yes, your shoes," I said.

"What's the problem?" Craig asked under his breath.

"I let them take off their shoes, and now they all look alike, and we don't know whose are whose."

"Yeah, that is quite a problem," he said, grinning. "But I think I have an idea. You tell me the kids' names, one by one."

I looked at the first name tag. "Gerry Smith," I said. Craig bent down and picked up a pair of sneakers. He looked inside them carefully. "Gerry Smith!" he called out in an authoritative voice. "These are Gerry Smith's all right."

Gerry took them and put them on without a murmur. Soon all twenty pairs were taken, and all the kids were running happily to their parents. Only Craig and Cindy were left.

"Come on, Craig, let's go," Cindy said, pulling on his hand. But Craig hesitated.

"Can I see you again, sometime?" he asked. "Without her, I mean."

"I'd like that," I managed to say calmly, even though my heart was racing.

"I wanted to see you before," he said, "but Bessie died."

"Oh, no! What happened?"

"She died of old age on the freeway. I'm still looking for a replacement I can afford."

"I'm sorry to hear about Bessie."

"Me, too. She was like one of the family. But I guess I'll get over it. Hey, do you like music? Classical music, I mean?"

"Believe it or not, I do."

"That's fantastic. There's this concert in the park on Saturday night, sort of pop classical. Would you like to go? I think my mother might lend me her car."

"I'd like that very much."

"Come on, Craig, I want to go home," Cindy insisted. She pulled hard at his hand, dragging him away.

"I'll pick you up on Saturday about seven, OK?"

"Terrific."

"Your number's thirty-five, isn't it?"

"Right."

"Great. Bye, Jill."

"Bye, Craig."

"And beware of identical sneakers from now on," he called as he was dragged across the school yard.

Chapter Thirteen

Have you ever had a week with five hundred days in it—and each day with at least a thousand hours? That was how long my week seemed until my Saturday date with Craig. Even my busy days at camp did not make the week go by more quickly. I had hoped to see him after school each day when he picked up Cindy. But at the end of the next day, Cindy ran across to a green station wagon. I caught a glimpse of a woman with elegant gray hair as they drove off. I guessed that must have been Craig's mother.

I did have the courage to ask Cindy where Craig was one day, and she said he was working. Then she had the nerve to ask me if I liked him. I said of course I liked him. Then she laughed and asked me why my cheeks were red, so I avoided that subject in the future. I did not intend to be teased by all those first graders!

My evenings were busy, too. Every night I went through my wardrobe trying to decide what to wear on my date with Craig. What did people wear to an outdoor concert, for heaven's sake? I didn't want to be the only person wearing jeans, but I didn't want to be the only person in a long dress, either. It was at times like this that I most missed Toni. It would have been such fun sharing my worries and excitement with her, letting her style my hair in lots of different ways to match my various outfits. But I hadn't seen her since the fight. I hadn't even heard any news about her. It was as if Toni Redmond had ceased to exist.

Several times I had to stop myself from going to the phone to call her. Over the years she had become as much a part of my life as eating and sleeping. Something funny would happen at camp, or there would be a good program on TV, and my first thought would be: I've got to tell Toni about this. I missed her terribly and was almost at the point of calling to apologize, but I didn't know what to say about the contest, especially since Craig had come into my life.

But toward the end of the week, thoughts of Toni were pushed out of my mind by more important things. My date was only two days away, and I still didn't know what to wear!

"Something pretty," my mother said. Normally that alone would have made me choose my dirtiest overalls, but for once I had a feeling she was right. I wanted Saturday night to be really special.

So I went to my closet and picked out the prettiest dress I owned. I had gotten it as a birthday present the year before but had hardly worn it since, because it was so dressy. But as I looked at myself in the mirror while I waited for Craig to pick me up, I was quite satisfied with what I saw. The dress was mid-calf length and white with tiny blue flowers on it. The front was tucked with panels of white ribbon, the skirt was edged with white lace, and so was the low neckline, which looked good with my tan. The sleeves were long, full and romantic, ending in tight wristbands buttoned with tiny pearls. As a finishing touch, I swept back my hair and caught it up on one side with a mass of white and blue ribbons.

The whole outfit was like something out of

a fantasy, and I couldn't help feeling like Cinderella waiting for the ball to begin.

When the doorbell rang, I felt a moment of panic. What if he was in jeans and a T-shirt and the concert was canceled and we were going bowling instead and he had forgotten to tell me? I opened the door, and there was Craig in a nice blue shirt that matched the color of his eyes and blue dress pants, looking just the way Prince Charming should. The look in his eyes told me that I had made the right choice in wearing the dress.

"You look terrific, Jill," he said.

I noticed that we both got some admiring glances as we walked across the park to the concert area. I felt so excited that my feet hardly touched the grass.

Craig spread out a blanket close to the stage, and we talked while we waited for the concert to begin. With Craig, there was no "making conversation" as there had been with so many other boys. We just wanted to know all about each other, and our questions and answers flew back and forth. In the space of those few minutes I learned about his family, his four sisters—all too smart for their own good and little pests according to him—and more about his aims for college and a career.

We talked about my family, my older sister,

my lonely only-child situation at home now. Craig said it sounded great to him.

"If you think it's bad not having someone to share secrets with, you should try finding a free bathroom in the morning. Then you'd see if sisters were such a good idea, especially when you finally get in and find out they'd used the last of your toothpaste!"

I laughed. "Well, my sister makes me babysit. There's nothing worse than that."

"Well, how about when they listen in to your private phone calls on the extension phone, and afterward they tease you about it: 'Ooooh, Craig talked to a girl!' "

"Do you do that often—talk to girls, I mean?"

"If you mean do I have a girlfriend right now, the answer's no. I had a girlfriend all through my senior year, but we broke up," he said, playing with a stalk of grass. "I really liked her, but she wanted to date other guys as well as me. I just couldn't handle that. I didn't want to date anyone else, and I couldn't figure out why she did."

Then the musicians came on stage and stopped that conversation from developing any further.

The concert was beautiful—full of haunting, romantic pieces that floated across the park like magic and made you feel your heart would break. Craig sat beside me on the blanket, close but not touching. I didn't know whether he was shy or just polite, but I wished he would hold my hand or something. I didn't want to push him, though. By the time the intermission came, we still hadn't touched, even though I could tell by the way he looked at me that he wanted to.

Actually we did touch for a moment during the intermission. We decided to walk around and stretch our legs. Craig took my hand to help me up. But he released it as soon as I was standing. We wandered through the twilight of the park. Trees loomed up like dragons and monsters in the fading light. A chill breeze sprang up. I shivered.

"Let's go back," he said. "You're cold." But he didn't put his arm around me as I hoped he would.

I had a sudden vision that this date would end like all the rest. Another washout. Another nondate to add to my summer full of nondates.

We settled back on our blanket. The music began again. I leaned back to look at the stars, but there weren't any. Without warning the chill breeze turned into a wild wind that raced across the park, snatching music from stands and programs from spectators. Everywhere people were yelling and laughing and grabbing for their things. But the musicians played steadfastly on.

The wind died as quickly as it had sprung up, and people had just begun to pay attention to the concert again when the rain came. No warning drops falling one by one. A solid downpour drenched us through right away. People pushed each other as they rushed for shelter. I scrambled to my feet, but a tremendous blow in the middle of my back sent me sprawling forward again onto the grass.

"Hey, lady, watch where you're going," I heard Craig shout angrily. Then he was lifting me up gently. "Are you all right?"

"I think so," I said shakily. "A little muddy, maybe. What happened?"

"Somebody came charging up behind you with a picnic basket. You met the picnic basket!" He smiled at me and grabbed my hand. "Come on, let's get out of here before we get washed away."

We snatched up the blanket and ran. We ran until we came to a huge tree that spread like a giant umbrella over the grass. We stood there, dripping and panting. We could hear the rain pattering on the tree-roof above us, but where we stood was dry—a private little world.

"I think we got a little wet," Craig said. I

had been worried about getting my dress covered with mud, but now, as I looked at Craig standing there like a drowned rat, his hair plastered to his face, I began to laugh.

"What the well-dressed concertgoer is wearing this year," I said.

Craig looked at himself, then at me, and started to laugh, too. We stood under the tree and laughed like lunatics.

"I must look like a total disaster," I finally said.

Craig reached out a finger and stroked my hair back from my cheek. "You look just fine," he said.

"I do?"

"In fact, you look beautiful," he said. His fingers slipped down under my chin as he drew my face toward him. His lips barely brushed mine, but I felt as if I had been struck by lightning.

"Is this OK, Jill?" he asked seriously.

"It's very OK," I whispered as our lips met for the second time. This time it was not a gentle brush. Craig may have been shy, but he sure knew how to kiss a girl once he decided it was all right to.

"I was going to ask you to go out for something to eat after the concert," he said when we drew apart, "but I think we might get some strange looks if we went into a restaurant looking like this. What's more, you're shivering, so we'll save that for next time."

Then we drove home. Personally, I didn't need the car. I was floating several feet above the ground and could have wafted myself home with no effort at all.

All the way home I kept rerunning his words through my head like a tape:

"We'll save that for next time. We'll save that for next time. . . ."

It was wonderful to realize that there was really going to be a next time.

Chapter Fourteen

It wasn't until I was playing a counting game at camp the next day that I remembered about Toni and the ten-boy bet. But somehow it didn't seem to matter anymore.

Toni can go ahead and date every boy in Seattle as far as I'm concerned, I thought. *Let her win her stupid bet. Craig is much more important than winning any dumb bet.*

I couldn't feel angry at Toni, though. I had a bad case of love, and it changed my entire outlook on life. The little brats at camp changed into adorable little angels who brought me flowers and asked me all sorts of sweet questions. I patted them all on the head and smiled all day.

Cindy wasn't at camp that day, so I wasn't

expecting to see Craig. But he materialized just as I was sending off the last little angel with a big hug.

"A very touching scene," he observed as I straightened up.

"If you've come for your sister, she isn't here today," I said.

"I didn't come for Cindy. I came for you," he said, taking my hand as if it were the most natural thing in the world. "It's a nice afternoon. Let's go for a drive somewhere."

"What happened to Cindy?" I asked as we walked to the car.

"She doesn't feel well, and she's running a fever."

"Poor kid. It could be chicken pox," I said. "We've had three cases of it at camp this week."

"Well, she wasn't spotty when I left home," Craig said.

"I hope you're not infectious," I teased as we climbed into the car.

"We'll see," he said, as his lips came toward mine.

Craig had some errands to do for his mother, which was the reason he had her car all afternoon. After the last errand, we drove along by the water, walked along the beach, picked up shells, and threw rocks into the ocean.

We finished up the afternoon at my house. My mother, of course, thought Craig was "such a nice boy." It got sort of embarrassing the way she kept complimenting him.

"Don't come on too strong or you'll scare him away," I whispered when she and I were in the kitchen.

But she didn't scare him away. He was waiting for me the next afternoon after camp, even though there was no Cindy to pick up.

"You were right," he said. "It was chicken pox. She's now covered from head to toe. She looks terrible, but she's actually feeling better and is bugging all of us to play Atari games with her."

"Poor little thing, I ought to come see her," I said, showing what a great counselor I had turned into.

"Are you sure you've had chicken pox?" Craig asked, looking worried.

"Pretty sure. I remember lying in bed and having spots when I was about four or five. That must have been chicken pox, right? And besides, we've had lots of other cases at camp. If I was going to get it, I would have come down with it already."

So I went with Craig to visit Cindy. I was the soul of patience, as she beat me at every Atari game, out-powing, out-shooting, and annihilating me with her spaceships. But it wasn't a wasted afternoon. I met another of Craig's sisters. Caroline, who was twelve, thought I was "real pretty and much prettier than Sheri" (who I gathered was Craig's previous girlfriend). I also met his mother and was a bit scared of her. She was tall and silver-haired and elegantly dressed. But she seemed to like me and was really nice.

After a blissful week with Craig, I felt full of love for the whole world, even my family. So I actually volunteered to take the family car and get it washed and filled up with gas on Saturday morning. My parents looked at each other as if I were crazy, and my mother said, "Are you sure you feel all right?"

"Just because I do one nice thing for you out of the goodness of my heart, you don't need to act as if I've flipped," I said haughtily and walked out of the room.

"It's that nice Craig," I heard my mother say. "He's such a good influence on her."

I drove downtown to the Rainbubble, where you can get the car washed for a dollar with a fill-up.

"Fill it with unleaded," I said to the station attendant. Then I did a double-take. The station attendant was Toni. Dressed in blue-and-white striped overalls, she looked cuter than ever. More like something out of a Hollywood movie in which the star discovers the girl of his dreams working at a gas station and they do a tap dance routine together.

"Oh, hi," I said uneasily.

"Hi," she said in an expressionless voice. Then she deliberately turned her back on me as she pumped the gas.

"Did you want the car wash, too?" she asked as she took my credit card.

"Sure."

"Then pull around onto the track and switch off your engine," she said.

She spoke to me as if I were a total stranger. I felt a lump in my throat. I wanted to get out and shake her, tell her to stop being so childish and be friends again. Why was she being so stubborn and acting this way?

I swung the car around onto the track and switched off the engine. Toni came around to the side of the car.

"How are you doing on your list?" she asked.

"I've given that up. It was pretty childish, anyway."

"Couldn't make it, eh? Well, for your information, I'm already up to number seven. I've already seen the pair of jeans I want. They're purple and very expensive. I'm glad I'm going to get them without any competition. You always were a chicken, I guess."

I knew there was no way I could talk sense to her, but at that moment I also missed her more than ever. I decided that for the sake of our friendship, I would just have to get back into the contest. But what about Craig?

"Don't be too sure of yourself, Toni," I finally said. "I've already had several dates with my mystery man. Don't count me out of the race yet."

She looked at me quickly to see if I really meant it, and I think she almost smiled.

"May the best girl win," I said and drove away.

Chapter Fifteen

The problem was: how could I date seven boys without Craig knowing about them? It seemed pretty impossible. Besides, I didn't want to date any other boys at all since I'd met Craig. But I also didn't want to lose Toni as a friend. After all, I decided, they could be nice harmless dates. But where did I find them?

"I'll just have to meet them places Craig doesn't go," I said to myself and proceeded to make a list of them. He didn't belong to my parents' tennis club so that was number one on the list. The pool there might be a good place to pick up boys. He belonged to a different branch of the public library, and boys had been known to have been found there.

But after that, my mind was a blank. My experience with the octopus-armed guys warned me not to look for boys at places like discos or roller rinks.

I waited until Craig had an afternoon modeling job, and after work I went down to the pool in my new yellow bikini. Then I lay down in the sun, on my bright blue towel. I'd been there about an hour before anyone paid any attention to me. He was tall and very muscular and had a mass of blond curls.

"I haven't seen you here before," he said.

"That's because I've been working all summer," I said.

He smiled. "My name's Brent," he said.

Wheels churned in the back of my brain. "Not Brent Masterson?"

"Yeah—how did you know?"

"I'm Jill Gardner. We used to fight while our parents played tennis."

"You? Little Jill Gardner? The skinny one with freckles?"

"That's me."

"Boy, have you grown up!" he said, looking at me admiringly.

"You've changed a bit yourself," I said.

He grinned. "I'm on my college swim team in Los Angeles. All that working with weights has turned me into Mr. Universe overnight!"

I couldn't believe my luck. I wanted a date, and I had found a long-lost friend who had turned into the cutest boy for miles around. What's more, he invited me to a barbeque with his friends that evening.

He was fun to be with, and his friends were great—so why did I feel so miserable? I saw them all laughing and having a good time, and all I could think of was Craig. When Brent kissed me, I felt nothing except that his lips were not Craig's lips. At the end of the evening, Brent asked to see me again. I realized then that I'd really been misleading him and could have really hurt his feelings. I apologized and told him about Craig.

He was very nice about it and said my boyfriend was a lucky guy and to give him a call if we ever broke up. So we parted on good terms. Afterward, of course, I felt terrible. This wasn't going to work at all. I just couldn't date other guys when I felt the way I did about Craig. It wasn't fun for me, and it wasn't fair to them.

I was really depressed about the whole situation until the next day, when I cycled down to the library after work to return some books for my mother. Who should I run into but good old Eric, my long-lost steady. He looked up from a book, which was, no doubt, about the sex life of the lesser wolf spider of Albania, and his face broke into a big smile when he saw me.

"How's it going, Jill?"

So I had to sit down and tell him all the details of my summer—about my jobs, that is. I left out all the details of my private life. Then I politely asked him about his summer.

"You'll never guess," he said with enthusiasm. "My dad's just bought a minicomputer for the house. It's fantastic. You can play chess with it and make colored designs. It's even programmed for Space Invaders."

"That's great, Eric," I said, thinking how lucky I was that I was not tied to a Space Invaders freak for the entire summer.

"Hey, you want to come and see it tonight?" he asked.

I was about to find a prior engagement when I thought again. Three hours with Eric, playing Space Invaders, would count as a date! I could even arrange a quick peck on the cheek at the end, for old times' sake, just to make it legal. After all, Toni had made no rules about dating former boyfriends. And there was no way I could hurt Eric's feelings. By the way he was looking at me, I could tell I was just a Space Invaders partner to him, not the love of his life.

"Sure, Eric," I said. "I'd love to come!"

So now I was up to five, without really trying. But even though I knew my dates were harmless—well, almost harmless—I still had a nagging twinge of guilt when I thought about Craig.

When I got home from Eric's, I went up to my room and turned on the TV. There was an old movie on. A woman in a slinky dress was pacing up and down in a mansion.

"How could you pretend to love me, Richard," she asked in a clipped English voice, "when all the time you were seeing another? Why didn't you have the decency to tell me it was over between us instead of letting me go on hoping. . . ."

Doubts began to creep into my mind. Unseeing, I sat in front of the TV. Why hadn't Craig called me for several days? Why was he out late every night? Could anyone really have to work that late? Or was it an excuse? Had he seen me with Brent or Eric?

I sat there torturing myself, feeling more and more depressed. I had never felt this way before. Eric had given me a warm, comfortable feeling, but nothing like the agony and ecstasy I felt when I thought about Craig. If Eric had told me he couldn't make a date, the world wouldn't have fallen apart.

Before Eric, I'd had some dates and crushes but nothing, nothing like this. Nothing had prepared me for being really and truly in love, for feeling that my heart might break with happiness one minute or with despair the next. I hadn't realized until now how very special Craig was to me—not just because he was great-looking and interesting and fun to be with, but just because I couldn't bear to think about life without him.

I turned off the English movie, having decided that Cynthia was a stupid woman who deserved to lose Richard anyway. Then I went to bed and cuddled Teddy Blue, something I hadn't done for a long time.

I came back from a deep sleep to hear someone calling to me. "Phone call, Jill!"

For a moment I wondered who would be calling me in the middle of the night, but then I saw it was only around eleven. I had only been asleep for a few minutes. I rushed downstairs.

"Jill, I hope I didn't wake you," said Craig.

"Oh, er, no, Craig. I was just watching an old movie on TV," I lied.

"Well, I'm sorry to be calling you up so late," he said. "But it seems like we haven't talked to each other for ages, and I was lonesome for the sound of your voice."

Suddenly the world turned into a wonderful, magical place again. "You were?" I asked.

"Every minute. But this job—well, it's not like working regular hours. I have to work when I get work, and this week we're doing a whole winter catalog. You can just imagine me stomping around in my fur-lined boots, dripping with sweat inside my parka, and thinking, 'Today I'll be through in time to see Jill.' Then the photographer says we need one more retake, and my evening vanishes before my eyes."

"Poor Craig," I said. "But think of all that money you're making."

"I am thinking about it. It's what keeps me going when they want me to stand in the glaring sun in full ski gear. And you know what? I've almost got enough to buy a new Bessie."

"That's great, Craig. I wish making peanut butter sandwiches and wiping noses paid that much."

"Hey, Jill, I wanted to ask you something. Are you free tomorrow night? We've almost finished with the catalog. I really think I might be free by around six. Let's go out and celebrate, OK?"

"I'd really like that."

"Wear your pretty dress," Craig said. "We're

going somewhere special. I'll pick you up around seven. Well, I think I'll collapse from exhaustion now. Good night, Jill. Sleep tight."

"Good night, Craig."

I crawled back to bed feeling warm and comforted. I even put Teddy Blue back on the shelf.

"Sorry, old pal," I said, "but I don't think I need you after all."

Chapter Sixteen

The next evening Craig was there at seven o'clock on the dot. Luckily, I was ready to go. I'd even put my hair up this time, something I hardly ever did because my hair is heavy and it takes me so long.

"I feel like I'm going out with a sophisticated woman tonight," Craig teased. "But you must be psychic. That hairdo is just right for where we're going."

Now I was curious. "Where *are* we going?"

"You'll see," he said, looking smug.

We drove in near silence. But it wasn't a frosty silence. It was the silence of being comfortable together, and his right hand was in mine.

We drove down toward the docks, along the

harbor, and finally stopped outside a big, elegant building. It was built right out over the water and was almost all glass so that light spilled down onto the black water below. From inside came the sound of a piano. A couple pulled up beside us in a white Mercedes. The man jumped out to open a door for the woman. She climbed out looking like something out of a fashion magazine. They disappeared into the building.

"Come on," Craig said. "What are we waiting for?"

"We're going in there?"

"Well, we didn't come down here for a little night fishing!"

"But, Craig, it looks awfully expensive."

He smiled. "I'll let you in on a secret. This is a place I did an advertisement for. The owner wrote me a letter and invited me to bring a date to dinner. So it's all on the house."

We went in, but I couldn't stop feeling nervous. My family never ate in places like this. The maître d' who showed us to our table looked like the French ambassador.

"Would monsieur like to look at the wine list?" he asked.

"Thank you, but we'll just have water with our meal," Craig said. I beamed at him in admiration for the way he had carried that off. I would have mumbled something about not being eighteen yet.

Then someone brought us the menu. It was all in French. I stared at it blankly, wishing I hadn't chosen Spanish in my freshman year.

"I'll have what you have," I said.

"I wish I knew what I was going to have," Craig said, and for the first time I got a hint that he felt strange and a little scared, too.

"You're ready to order, monsieur?" asked a voice. Another waiter had arrived.

"Er—we haven't quite—that is—" Craig stuttered. But the waiter suddenly looked as if he understood.

"Ah, since it is monsieur's first visit here, might I suggest the sole stuffed with crabmeat. It is one of our specialties, and I think you will both enjoy that."

"Thank you," we both said and looked gratefully at him.

"And to go with it," he went on, "may I suggest just a simple green salad, tossed with the chef's special dressing, our tiny shoestring french fries, and perhaps a little broccoli?"

We both nodded, and the waiter went away looking satisfied, as if he were an overage boy scout who had done his good deed.

"How are you enjoying it so far?" Craig asked.

I leaned forward. "To tell you the truth, I'm scared. I can feel all those people staring at us, saying 'What are a couple of kids doing here? They don't belong in a place like this.' "

"Yeah, I feel the same way," Craig said. "Even the waiters look distinguished. You want to sneak out right now and get some pizza instead?"

I smiled. "We wouldn't dare. We'd never get past the French ambassador at the door."

So we sat and waited for what seemed like an awfully long time. The piano player got through a couple of complete Broadway shows. I drank all of my ice water, and Craig drew lines on the white linen tablecloth with his fork. Then something cold slid down my neck, and I realized it was a hairpin.

That does it, I thought. *All I need is for my hair to start falling down while all those people watch.*

So I excused myself and walked, without moving my head one inch, to the powder room. That was an eye-opener, too! The walls were quilted satin. The sinks were white marble with glass faucets. On the floor was a thick white carpet that you absolutely sank into. It looked like the bedroom from some old Hollywood movie. It took me ages to put my hair up again because with all those mirrors, I kept seeing another wisp of hair escaping somewhere.

At last I came out and gave Craig a big smile as I sat down again.

"Dinner's still not here?" I asked. "I bet they went out to catch the fish!" Then I stopped suddenly because I noticed his face. He looked sick.

"What's wrong?" I asked. "You don't look so hot."

"Jill," he whispered. "I just discovered I—uh—"

"You what?"

This was the moment the waiter chose to bring us our fish. "Here we are, mademoiselle, cooked to perfection," he said as he put the plate in front of me. "Enjoy your dinner."

"Wow, this looks good," I said. I was starving and couldn't wait a second longer. I cut into the stuffed sole and chewed on a delicious mouthful. "And you know what? It tastes as good as it looks! Why don't you start? Maybe you'll feel better with a little dinner inside you."

"I doubt that," he said. "What I was trying to tell you was that I don't have the letter inviting us for a free dinner."

"Well, that's not the end of the world," I said. "Just ask to see the manager afterward and explain."

"But what if the manager doesn't know anything about this? What if he's not here tonight and no one knows anything about me? It was the owner who invited me, and he's away on a cruise."

"Oh."

We both looked down at our plates, both thinking the same thoughts. Would we be thrown out? Arrested? Would we have to work off our meal by washing dishes? Would there be a horrible scene with all those elegant people turning to stare at us?

Suddenly the fish didn't taste so good.

"I have about ten dollars on me," I said.

"And I have about fifteen," Craig said. "But judging by these prices, that's not nearly enough."

"Maybe they'd take it as a deposit," I said.

Suddenly he grinned. "It'll all work out," he said. "It's got to. Let's just enjoy our dinner before it gets cold. It might be the only time in our whole lives we can afford to eat in a place like this."

We both tried to enjoy it. It was hard not to because the food was so delicious. But we both refused the dessert, even though the cherries jubilee sure looked tempting.

Now came the moment of truth. The waiter brought us the bill. Craig asked in a low voice to see the manager. The manager came. Heads turned at all the other tables. My cheeks went crimson. Craig took a deep breath and began.

"My name is Wexler," he said.

"Wexler?" the manager said. "Wexler. Ah, yes. We were told to expect you. I hope you enjoyed your dinner here, sir."

Then we left. We were both still shaking a little at the knees, but we managed to walk past the maître d' with great dignity. We kept walking silently and seriously to the car. Then, as we drove away, we looked at each other and burst out laughing.

"Craig, you were fantastic!" I said. "You stayed so calm."

"Well, you were fantastic, too," he said. "You didn't panic, either."

Suddenly he stopped the car. "Jill, there's something I want to tell you," he said. "Remember I told you that last year I got very involved with a girl at school? I cared about her a lot. I thought she felt the same about me. She acted as though she did. But then I found out she had been dating other guys all year, behind my back, and everyone else knew about it except me. After that, I decided I'd never feel that way about anyone else again. I've had a few casual dates since then, but I always back off before it gets serious."

I felt myself go cold all over. *He's trying to tell me it's over,* I thought. *He wants to leave me before it gets serious—or else he saw me with Eric or Brent and got the wrong idea!*

"Jill," he said, taking my hand, "I want you to know that you are very special to me. When I decided those things, I never dreamed I'd meet you. I know now that it's serious with us, whether I want it to be or not. And I have to know how you feel about me. . . ."

"Craig, I've never been in love before," I said at last, "never really in love. But I know that this is the real thing."

Then we kissed. On the way home I decided *no more Toni, no more dates. Nothing matters in the whole world but Craig.*

Chapter Seventeen

Of course, having sworn never to date another boy as long as I lived, the perfect opportunity came up the same week—so perfect that even I could not turn it down. I don't want to sound like a complete jerk who goes behind my boyfriend's back, so let me say right now that this isn't as bad as it sounds. . . .

I had a terrible day at camp. The kids had been super annoying. One kept crying for no reason at all. One got lost on a hike. By the end of the day I had a bad headache. The weather was still unusually hot and sticky, and I had to cycle home.

I was puffing and panting as I cycled up the steep hill near our house when a motorbike drew up beside me.

"Hi, stranger!" the motorcyclist called.

I looked around to see if he was calling anyone else, but the street was empty except for me. Then he took off his helmet. It was Toni's oldest brother, Steve.

"Haven't seen you in a while," he said.

"Toni and I had a fight."

"So I heard," he said, grinning. "I wish you two would make up again. She's in a rotten temper all the time."

"It's not up to me to make up," I said.

"That's exactly what she said."

"Well, give my regards to your mother and the others," I said. "I have to be getting on home." My head was throbbing, and all I could think of was grabbing a cool drink and going to bed.

I started to cycle away, but soon I heard the roar of the motorbike again, and Steve drew up beside me.

"Wait, Jill, I've just had a thought. We're going to the fair tonight. Just us three guys. You want to come with us?"

I was about to refuse. After all, a carnival was the last place I felt like going at the moment. Then the thought suddenly struck me. This was the ideal way of staying in the contest. I could make this count as three dates. Even Toni would get a laugh out of it when she found out. It was too good a chance to turn down, even for a bad headache. It didn't even occur to me that Craig might not approve. After all, these were just like my brothers. I had known them since I was seven, and they all treated me like a kid sister.

"That sounds like fun," I said.

"Great," he said. "I'll be around to pick you up at six."

The carnival was better than most years. The midway was full of exciting rides. There was one that flung you around and almost broke your neck. There was another that turned you over and over and around and around at the same time. There was a very fast roller coaster. And there was a haunted house. I went into the haunted house with Will, the youngest, and he put an arm around me so that I wouldn't feel scared. I snuggled close to Steve on the roller coaster, and I held on to Pete when we were left hanging upside down on the Dive Bomber.

After we had ridden the roller coaster three times, we went to have hot dogs. Before we started, I had taken a couple of aspirins for my headache and had been feeling pretty good for a while. Now, quite suddenly, the headache returned, much worse than before. The whole midway swayed in front of my eyes.

"Look, guys, I don't feel too good," I said. "I think I'll go and sit down somewhere for a while."

I felt more terrible from minute to minute—hot and clammy one second and cold and shivery the next. Steve looked at me with concern.

"You look awful," he said. "Maybe we shouldn't have ridden that roller coaster three times in a row. Come on, we'll go find somewhere for you to sit."

He took my arm and pushed his way through the crowd. The music of the merry-go-round, screams from the roller coaster, the sweet smell of cotton candy, onions from the hamburger stand, the flashing lights—all spun nightmarishly in my head. Then suddenly, through my nightmare, I felt someone grabbing my arm.

"Jill, hey, what a surprise. What are you doing here?"

My eyes focused painfully on Craig—Craig looking happy and relaxed in a T-shirt and shorts, smiling at me.

"Oh, Craig," I said unsteadily, "hi."

"Hi." He laughed. "You look kind of shaky. Did you just ride one of those awful things?"

"No, I mean, yes. I just don't feel too good right now."

"You want me to take you home?" he asked, his face full of concern.

I was about to say yes, but before I could get the words out, I heard Steve behind me saying, "It's OK. I'm just taking her to sit down for a while."

Craig eyed Steve up and down. "Who are you?" he asked.

My head was fuzzy, and my legs didn't want to hold me up any longer. Why I didn't just say, "He's my friend's brother," I'll never know. Instead, I heard myself mumbling, "Oh, he's my cousin from Ohio."

I looked at Steve, willing him to play along. But Steve was never one of the brightest of the Redmonds. He thought I was playing a joke.

"I'm supposed to be your what?" he asked, grinning stupidly.

Craig's eyes narrowed. "I see," he said. "It certainly didn't take you long to decide you didn't like waiting at home for me."

"Craig, you don't see at all," I pleaded. "It's not like that. . . . I thought—"

"You thought I'd be at work tonight," he said bitterly. "I know all about that one. I *was* at work, too, until half an hour ago.

Then the guy I was driving home with wanted to stop off here. I'd ask your friend to take you home, if I were you. You look terrible." Then he turned his back on me and pushed his way roughly through the crowd.

"Craig, wait," I yelled after him, but my words were swallowed up by the sounds of the fair.

"What was that all about?" Steve asked, looking confused.

"I just lost the most wonderful boy in the world," I said. "Do you think you could take me home now?"

"Sure," he said. "If we can fight our way through this mob." Steve was a football player, and he did a good job of pushing people out of the way for me. It was the last Saturday of the fair, and everyone in town seemed to be there, everyone including . . .

"Well, look who's here," Toni yelled as she saw us. She walked over to us, dragging behind her a dark-haired boy I had never met before.

"Hi, Jill," she said very sweetly. "I'd like you to meet Eduardo. He's number eight."

She smiled, the sweetest, cutest smile. "And how are you getting along these days? Don't tell me you're so hard up for dates that you have to sink to my brothers?"

All the time she talked I was feeling worse and worse. The lights above me were turning around and around. All I wanted to do was lie down and go to sleep. I made a supreme effort. "Toni," I said, and I tried to sound calm and reasonable, "I am also on number eight, but I want you to know that you don't have to try anymore. I have just lost the only boy I've ever really cared about because of this stupid contest. It's wrecked our friendship, and it's brought me nothing but trouble. I hereby announce finally, forever, and once and for all that I *quit*. You are officially declared the winner. Send the bill for the jeans to my house and leave me alone."

I expected Toni to start one of her yelling matches, but she did nothing but stare at me with her mouth open. "Jill," she said at last, "what's wrong with you?"

"What do you mean? Apart from a blinding headache and a fever of a hundred and five and a broken heart, I feel just fine. I've never felt better in my whole life."

"But your arms," she said. "They're all covered with spots."

"Oh," I said, looking down at them casually, as if they belonged to someone else. "That's funny. I probably have the plague as well as everything else. It wouldn't suprise me in the least."

Then I fainted.

Chapter Eighteen

When I opened my eyes, I was lying comfortably in my own warm bed. For a moment the ceiling swung around me, revealing a sea of worried faces that all looked comical upside down. One by one they brought themselves into focus: my mother, my father, my sister Stephanie, and Toni.

"If you've come for the reading of my will," I said to Toni, "I'm *not* leaving you my purple sweater."

"Thank heavens she's all right," my mother said, sitting down on the side of my bed. She reached out and took my hand. "You gave us all a nasty fright, honey."

"I did?" I tried to sit up and was immediately dazzled by the strong sunlight.

"How come the sun's shining?" I asked.

"It usually does at nine in the morning—on nice days, that is," Toni said.

"What happened to the night?" I had a vague recollection of being put to bed, of a lot of people around me, and of our family doctor sticking a thermometer into my mouth.

"You were delirious," my mother said, patting my hand as if I were two years old. "But Dr. Harris said that a high fever is quite usual in cases like yours."

"Cases of what?"

"Chicken pox," Toni said. "What did you think you had with all those spots?"

I looked at my arms. They were covered with horrible blisters. "I thought I had chicken pox when I was little," I said to my mother.

"It wasn't chicken pox," my mother said. "It turned out to be an allergic rash. Don't you remember?"

I didn't. I looked at my arms again. I had chicken pox. Suddenly I started to laugh. I laughed and laughed. Everyone stared at me as if I had finally flipped. In fact, my father and Steph said something to each other and tiptoed out. *They've probably gone for the straitjacket*, I thought.

Gradually my laughter subsided, and I realized something. "I'm hungry. What's for breakfast?"

"What would you like, honey?" my mother asked.

"I bet she'd like french toast and bacon," Toni said.

"I don't need you to answer for me," I said. "I'd like french toast and bacon, please. And anyway," I added, looking hard at Toni, "what is that person doing in my room?"

"Toni sat by your bed all last night," my mother said. "She was very worried about you." Then she went out, closing the door behind her.

"You were probably just worried that I'd die before I paid up for the designer jeans," I said bitterly.

"Jill," Toni said in a small voice—a very small voice for her. "I feel just terrible."

"So do I. Like one giant itch. Join the club."

"No, seriously. I feel just terrible about what I did—and said. It was stupid to fight over a dumb bet. I've been feeling bad ever since. . . . But you know me. I find it so hard to admit that I'm wrong. You're right, the whole bet was a ridiculous idea. And when you fainted at my feet last night, I realized you were

156

the best friend I ever had. Life's not the same without you. We belong together. We make a great team. So will you ever forgive me?"

I nodded. "I'll think about it."

"And let's be friends again?"

"I suppose so."

Then I remembered the worst part about last night. "Oh, Toni, what am I going to do? I fell in love with the most fantastic boy in the world, and because of our stupid bet, I tried to get my ten dates, and I thought he was at work, so I went to the fair with your brothers, and I didn't think there would be any harm in that, but he wasn't at work, and he saw me at the fair, and I said it wasn't your brother but my cousin from Ohio, and then he just walked away. . . ."

"Run that by me one more time," Toni said, "and slowly." I did. She listened in silence.

"Toni, what am I going to do? I really love him. He is the only boy I've ever loved in my whole life." A tear escaped from the corner of my eye. Then I couldn't stop more tears from coming.

"Just call him up and explain," Toni said. "I'm sure he'll understand. He'll realize that nobody in their right mind would want to date my brothers."

I shook my head. "I know he won't understand. He was let down badly once before. He trusted me, and I let him down again." I buried my head in the pillow, overcome with my own misery. I didn't even hear Toni creep out.

The day dragged on in an agony of itching and headache. The spots seemed to multiply every second. In fact, I passed the time staring at my body, seeing if I could actually watch new spots growing.

My eyes hurt too much to read, and my head hurt too much to watch TV. So I lay and watched the shadows of the leaves outside move across the ceiling. Toward evening Dr. Harris came again.

"Boy, do you ever look a mess," he said, chuckling.

"I didn't think doctors made house calls anymore," I said.

"Well, I certainly couldn't let you into my office in that state," he said. "You'd scare away all my other patients."

After he had gone, leaving behind an anti-itching prescription, I got up and looked at myself in the bathroom mirror. The sight was so horrible that it scared even me. It was like something out of a horror movie. Every surface of my skin was spotty. My eyelids were half swollen shut with spots. My lips were puffed out with spots. Any flesh in between the spots was deathly pale, and my eyes looked hollow and sunken, as if I were a survivor from a shipwreck. I was not a pretty sight, but the way I looked matched my mood—hopeless!

I staggered back to bed and lay staring at the ceiling again. The leaves on my ceiling danced a spooky dance in the light of the street lamp.

Then I heard footsteps coming up the stairs, the slow and steady feet of my father. He had gone to fill that anti-itching prescription. Now he would sit by my bed and make jokes and try to cheer me up as if I were a two-year-old. I didn't even want to see him. I pulled the sheets over my head and pretended I wasn't there as he came into the room.

"Go away," I said. "There's nobody here."

"Strange," said the voice. "I could swear the bulge under that sheet moved."

But it wasn't my father's voice.

"Craig?" I asked, wondering if I had relapsed into a fever and was hallucinating again.

"Well, it's not Santa Claus or the Tooth

Fairy," said the voice. "Aren't you going to come out and say hello?"

"You wouldn't want to see me like this," I said from under the sheet. "I look terrible."

"I've just been through the chicken pox with Cindy, remember? I think I'm brave enough to stand the sight."

Then he lifted the sheet gently away from my face.

"See," I said. "I told you I look terrible."

"Well," he said, "you certainly aren't looking your best tonight. I was going to kiss you, but I think I'll wait a day or so, if you don't mind." But he did sit down right beside me. "I hear you were pretty sick last night."

I nodded. "Craig, about last night—" I said, but he took my hand.

"Listen, I know all about last night. Your friend Toni came to my house this afternoon. I didn't want to talk to her at first, but she wouldn't go away until she had told me everything. I feel like a complete fool—getting jealous because you were at the fair with your friend's brothers. Why on earth didn't you tell me who the boy was?"

"I guess I was sick," I said lamely.

He smiled. "She's a pretty gutsy girl, isn't she—your friend Toni?"

160

I smiled, too. "Yeah, there's no one in the world quite like Toni."

"Oh, and by the way," Craig said, "she also told me all about your contest. Seems like it ended in a tie."

After he left, I called up Toni immediately. "Toni, you're the *best* best friend anyone could ever have! Thank you, thank you, thank you. I'll do anything you ask from now on, I promise."

"Sure, that's what you say now. Anyway, it was nothing. And I know exactly how you feel. I met somebody kind of special myself this summer."

"You did? Who? What's he like? And why didn't you tell me? I felt so guilty about Craig."

"Well, remember that guy Jeff I met when I was a maid? Well—we've kind of been going steady for most of the summer."

"Toni, how could you? Going steady? And you made me feel so rotten for wanting out of the bet! Why didn't you let me call it off?"

"I wanted to, but I just couldn't. I knew you'd never let me live it down. Besides, I just couldn't admit I'd really fallen in love."

"Oh, Toni, isn't it wonderful? I'm so happy!

I bet this summer will turn out to have been the best summer of our whole lives!"

"Please, Jill, no more bets! Now get some sleep and get over those chicken pox. I want you to look presentable when I introduce you to Jeff. Now good night."

"Good night, Toni, and thanks—for everything."

Chapter Nineteen

Two weeks later, I was riding with Craig in his new car—a bright blue VW bug at least five years younger than Bessie and christened Bessie-Too. Outside it was a perfect end-of-summer day—except that we were thinking about having to say goodbye.

Craig parked the car outside the park, and we took a blanket and sat down under our favorite tree.

"Just think," he said, "I leave for college in ten days. I hope Bessie-Too can stand the strain of commuting to visit you every week-end."

"Oh, Craig, I don't think I can stand the strain of not seeing you every day. This summer has just flown by."

"It's been a pretty good summer, though, hasn't it?"

"Oh, I don't know, I wouldn't call getting chicken pox pretty good, would you?" I teased.

"Besides the chicken pox, I mean," he said.

"Well, then there was Maxi's. That wasn't too wonderful."

"But you never would have met me if you hadn't been at Maxi's," Craig said softly as he reached for my hand.

"Hey, that's right. I really have Maxi to thank for all this. Let's drive by and I'll run in and give him a great big kiss."

"Jill, promise me you won't kiss anyone while I'm gone."

I looked at him seriously. "I really think I'm in love with you, Craig. But it probably wouldn't be fair to either of us to make any promises right now, would it? All we can do is wait and see if our love is going to last. I think it is, don't you?"

Then suddenly he was kissing me, and I knew that no matter what happened next year, Craig and I had found something real and special, and I would never, ever forget that magical, crazy summer as long as I lived.

of lies and confusion—until the night when her lies go too far.

#17 ASK ANNIE by Suzanne Rand
(#22518-9 • $1.95)

At first, Annie was thrilled to give Tim advice about his girlfriend—until he asks Annie how to keep beautiful, stuck-up Marcy in line. If she helps Tim keep Marcy, Annie will never get a chance with him. But if she doesn't, will Tim stop being her friend?

#18 TEN-BOY SUMMER by Janet Quin-Harkin
(#22519-7 • $1.95)

Jill's vacation gets off to a wild start when her best friend, Toni, thinks up a contest—who can be the first to date ten new boys! It seems like a great idea until Jill meets Craig and knows she's in love. If Jill drops out of the contest, she won't be able to face her best friend. If she doesn't, she'll lose Craig forever.

And make sure to look for these
Sweet Dreams romances, coming soon:

#19 LOVE SONG by Anne Park (*coming in August*)
#20 THE POPULARITY SUMMER by Rosemary Vernon (*coming in August*)
#21 ALL'S FAIR IN LOVE by Jeanne Andrews (*coming in September*)
#22 SECRET IDENTITY by Joanna Campbell (*coming in September*)
#23 FALLING IN LOVE AGAIN by Barbara Conklin
#24 THE TROUBLE WITH CHARLIE by Joan Lowery Nixon

STEP OUT OF YOUR WORLD AND ENTER THE

CIRCLE OF LOVE

Step into the lives of men who are true men...and true loves. Step into another country—another world. Step into the Circle of Love. You'll find Circle of Love romances unlike any other romance novel you've read. They're beautifully written. The stories are more memorable. The characters, more genuine. And the romance, more satisfying from beginning to end.

Receive Six Books Each Month for the Price of Four

Dear Reader:

With all the romance novels available, finding consistently satisfying reading is still not easy.

In Circle of Love romances, you're assured better writing. The stories are more suspenseful and more realistic. The characters are more genuine. And the romance is more satisfying from beginning to end.

Now you can enter the Circle of Love each month with the convenience of this no-risk offer.

Cordially,

Mary Harding

Mary Harding for Circle of Love

Membership Application

☐ **YES.** Please send me the next Circle of Love romances without obligation. If I decide to keep all six, I'll pay $7.95—the cost of 4 books plus postage. Then each month, I will receive six new titles at this same price.

SIGNATURE_____

NAME_____

ADDRESS_____

CITY_____ STATE_____ ZIP_____

Payment Options: (check one)

☐ **Charge each regular shipment to my:**   ☐ **Bill Me**
                                                      11023

13029 ☐ **Mastercard**   ☐ **VISA**

___*(Credit Card Number)*___   *expiration date*

Send no money now—but mail today to

Circle of Love Reader's Service, Bantam Books, P.O. Box 994,
Hicksville, N.Y. 11802

This offer is good only in the U.S. C 12